crazy for *you*

Here's all the dish on 'N Sync—Justin, JC, Joey, Chris, and Lance! Learn what their lives were like growing up in different parts of the country . . . how these five talented guys first came together . . . how they paid their dues, becoming a European pop sensation . . . and how they finally fulfilled their dream of making it big in the United States.

What's life like behind the scenes, at concerts, and on the road? Do the guys always get along? Where do they get their dazzling dance moves? How can *you* get in touch with them? Which member of 'N Sync would make the perfect boyfriend for you? Get all the info on the music scene's hottest new stars . . .

'N Sync

Look for other celebrity biographies from
Archway Paperbacks

Hanson: MMMBop to the Top by Jill Matthews
Isaac Hanson: Totally Ike! by Nancy Krulik
Taylor Hanson: Totally Taylor! by Nancy Krulik
Zac Hanson: Totally Zac! by Matt Netter
Hanson: The Ultimate Trivia Book! by Matt Netter
Jewel: Pieces of a Dream by Kristen Kemp
Jonathan Taylor Thomas: Totally JTT! by Michael-Anne Johns
Leonardo DiCaprio: A Biography by Nancy Krulik
Pop Quiz: Leonardo DiCaprio by Nancy Krulik
Matt Damon: A Biography by Maxine Diamond with Harriet Hemmings
Most Wanted: Holiday Hunks
'N Sync: Tearin' Up the Charts by Matt Netter
Pop Quiz by Nancy Krulik
Prince William: The Boy Who Will Be King by Randi Reisfeld
Will Power!: A Biography of Will Smith by Jan Berensen

For orders other than by individual consumers, Pocket Books grants a discount on the purchase of 10 or more copies of single titles for special markets or premium use. For further details, please write to the Vice-President of Special Markets, Pocket Books, 1633 Broadway, New York, NY 10019-6785, 8th Floor.

For information on how individual consumers can place orders, please write to Mail Order Department, Simon & Schuster Inc., 200 Old Tappan Road, Old Tappan, NJ 07675.

tearin' up the charts

An Unauthorized Biography

Matt Netter

POCKET BOOKS
New York London Toronto Sydney
Tokyo Singapore

AN ARCHWAY PAPERBACK *original*

An Archway Paperback published by
POCKET BOOKS, a division of Simon & Schuster Inc
1230 Avenue of the Americas, New York, NY 10020

ISBN: 0-671-03470-7

First Archway Paperback printing December 1998

10 9 8 7 6 5 4

Front cover photo by Todd Kaplan/Star File

Printed in the U.S.A.

IL 4+

To Michele, who deserves as much credit for this book as I do. Without her love and support I'd still be stuck on this page.

Special thanks to Jackie, Karen, and Melissa.

contents

introduction

The five young guys who call themselves 'N Sync love to travel, perform, and meet new people, which is a good thing, considering they've spent the past year spanning the globe doing just that. Along the way they've won over thousands of fans and stolen a lot of young hearts. While they were at it, they sold a few million records, topped the charts with hit singles, and packed concert arenas in cities all over the world. All in all 1998 was a magical year for a brand-new band consisting of five young guys living out their dreams.

Seventeen-year-old Tennessee native Justin Timberlake, Washington, D.C.–born JC Chasez, twenty-two, Mississippi's Lance "Lansten" Bass, nineteen, Pennsylvania-born Chris Kirkpatrick, twenty-seven, and native New Yorker Joey Fatone, twenty-one, came together in Orlando, Florida, seemingly by fate, to find that their varying personalities and considerable talents were in sync with one another's. After hooking up with legendary music manager Johnny Wright and then polishing their dance act through renowned choreographers, justiN, chriS, joeY, lansteN, and jC realized their true destiny—that they were 'N Sync.

A year of touring overseas got most of Europe hooked on the upbeat dance pop sounds of 'N Sync. "Tearin' Up My Heart" and "I Want You Back," their first two singles, made 'N Sync an instant hit in Germany, and before long, their debut album had gone gold in five different countries. The pop music fans in Great Britain couldn't get enough of 'N Sync, and in no time, the record went gold there as well. But how would America react to this wondrous pop-soul dance act?

In February 1998, 'N Sync released "I Want You Back" as their first single in North America, followed by their debut album in March. In Canada, the response was one of immediate enthusiasm. 'N Sync went platinum there in no time. In the U.S., where other pop groups, like the Backstreet Boys, were enjoying hard won success, 'N Sync seemingly had to pay their dues.

After 'N Sync introduced themselves through the media that spring in a flurry of press interviews, American fans started to react and their single began getting more radio play. Then, the group's big break happened. The Disney Channel wanted to air a concert special with the Backstreet Boys, but they were unavailable due to scheduling conflicts, and so 'N Sync was offered the chance to show off their voices and dance moves on TV for thousands of viewers. Well, thousands turned out to be millions as the special was one of the highest rated shows in the cable network's history. What was even better was that it helped 'N Sync win over droves of new fans, and suddenly their CDs began flying off the record store shelves and their single began climbing the charts.

By the end of that summer, 'N Sync's debut was certified platinum, "I Want You Back" went gold, and their second single, "Tearin' Up My Heart," quickly became one of the most played songs on the radio and most requested videos on cable music channels. The next few months would be among the busiest in the lives of

Justin, JC, Lance, Chris, and Joey. September was spent working on a Christmas album, making television appearances, doing major promotions, and later, in October, they filmed three holiday specials for television.

'N Sync closed out the year by going on their first American concert tour. The two-part tour featured a month of concerts in which the group opened for Janet Jackson and then another month in which they headlined. 'N Sync sold out arenas in more than a dozen U.S. cities, including three in their "home" state of Florida. Their now millions of fans enjoyed energetic stage performances from the group that featured wild acrobatics as part of their dance routines, as well as costume changes, special effects, cover songs, and audience sing-alongs.

By the end of the year, 'N Sync had very quickly become one of the most popular bands in the world. Suddenly, five nice American guys, who just a few years ago were going to high school or college and working in theme parks, were part of 'N Sync, a world-traveling, chart-topping, platinum-selling, arena-packing sensation. Now, if that's not living the American dream, what is?

So, who are these guys? How did they get together and how did they get their big break? What are they each like as individuals? Which 'N Sync guy would make the best boyfriend? What were their childhoods like? What's life like on the road for them and how are they handling success? What's the meaning and story behind their hit songs? Who do they look up to? What's in store for 'N Sync next year and beyond? You'll find the answers to all of these questions and many more right here in *'N Sync: Tearin' Up the Charts.*

1

the perfect blend

Although wildly famous pop quintet 'N Sync seemed to come out of nowhere to achieve fame and fortune in 1998, there is actually quite a story behind their rise to the top. It took the group nearly three years of rehearsing, choreographing, and promoting overseas to reach the mountain of stardom they now sit atop. And before that, fate brought five special young men together who exhausted every ounce of determination, pride, and sweat they could muster up to get the right manager, get a record deal, and, finally, get on the radio.

These five extraordinary guys came from different parts of America with very different backgrounds, but all with the same dream, to hit the big time in a pop band. How Justin Timberlake, JC Chasez, Chris Kirkpatrick, Joey Fatone, and Lance Bass united to form 'N Sync and realize their wildest dreams together reads like a game of Six Degrees of Kevin Bacon. Pay careful attention and try to follow along.

"It's a really long story how everybody met up," Justin warned a reporter who asked the guys in 'N Sync how they all met. "Basically, JC knew Joey before the group and I had also met Joey before the group. I knew Chris before the group too. Plus, I had the same vocal coach as Lance." That's it in a nutshell, but it gets a bit more complicated when you examine the situation more closely.

Justin, JC, & *The Mickey Mouse Club*

"We all had daydreams about being entertainers," Justin told reporters on hand for the taping of 'N Sync's Disney Channel special in the spring of 1998. My, how things have a way of coming full circle. Back in 1995, Justin was in his second season as a cast regular on The Disney Channel's long-running franchise *The Mickey Mouse Club*. Just two years earlier, Justin moved with his family to Orlando, Florida, from their home in Memphis, Tennessee, to accept the role.

The after-school club included twenty under-eighteen cast members as part of a variety show. The cast sang, danced, did comedy skits, and introduced guest stars. *The Mickey Mouse Club*, or *MMC* for short, was an entertaining and often educational show for millions of young viewers, but it was also a springboard for young talent. While Justin was part of the show, some of his cast mates included current TV stars Kerri Russell *(Felicity)* and Ryan Gosling *(Young Hercules)*, as well as three of today's upcoming pop music stars, Christina Aguilera, Brittany Spears, and JC Chasez.

It's no coincidence that so many stars emerged from *MMC*. Each year, thousands of hopefuls auditioned for the very few new parts on the show. "We spent a lot of energy and effort not to find just the most talented kids, but kids who'd be welcomed into the home every day," The Disney Channel's head of programming told *USA Today* back when the two boys were on *MMC*. JC was part of the show for four years, the last two of which were together with Justin.

JC and Justin became fast friends, finding they had a lot in common, especially that they both aspired to be professional musicians. Both young singer/dancers began working with the same vocal coach and, when their respective runs with *MMC* ended, they wound up in Nashville, Tennessee, simultaneously working on separate solo projects. Justin and JC began to realize they had similar singing styles and started thinking they could work together.

Chris & Joey

Meanwhile, back in Orlando, Joey Fatone, a talented young singer/dancer from New York, was working as a stage performer at Universal Studios theme park. Joey happened to be a friend of JC's. "Justin and I worked together, but I actually knew Joey two or three years before I knew Justin," JC told *16* magazine. "Being down in Orlando, you're bound to run into people. Joey and I met each other because he used to go to high school with Jennifer McGill who was on *The Mickey Mouse Club*. That's how we met and we've been friends for like seven years."

Joey had befriended a co-worker at Universal Studios who was a bit older than he was, but equally talented and ambitious. Of course, we're talking about Pittsburgh native Chris Kirkpatrick, who also was making a living singing and dancing for tourists at Universal. "Well, it all started with me," Chris told *Teen Beat* magazine. "I used to sing in coffee shops and I decided to take it real seriously and do this as a living, so I called up a couple of my friends, who are these guys. I called Justin, who worked with JC on *The Mickey Mouse Club*. That's how they knew each other, and I worked with Joey at Universal Studios."

JC elaborated to *Tiger Beat* magazine, "Everybody knew each other in a roundabout way, it was just a matter of the order that everybody called each other. But, Chris was the one who came up with the idea of the group." This is an important fact in the short history of 'N Sync. Many people mistakenly assume JC is the founder and leader of the group, but he's so darn modest, as you'll learn later, that he'd never dream of taking any undue credit.

When 'N Sync was on *Live! with Regis & Kathie Lee,* Chris was asked if he actually auditioned each member for the group. He joked, "If I had, I don't think Joey would have made it."

Speaking of Joey, here's his take on how the group came together. "We met at different times," he explained to a fan during an interactive Q&A session in Disney World. "I've known JC ever since I moved here six years ago. I used to go to high school with some of the people who were on *The Mickey Mouse Club* and he was on it. I met Chris about four years ago from working at Universal Studios. I knew Justin about two years prior to that and Lance was basically the only one I didn't know."

"We really put ourselves together," Justin told *Billboard* magazine in an interview that would take place three years and millions of fans later. "It's funny to look back on how well we all came together; it just happened step by step."

Functioning as a Foursome

By the summer of 1995, Joey, Chris, JC, and Justin all banded together down in Orlando as a singing and dancing quartet. While the four had such different backgrounds they all shared the same passion for performing and the hunger to succeed. They went over musical tastes and styles, discussed their dreams, and spent long hours in a nearby warehouse, working on their harmonizing and dancing.

"For the first year we were together we were struggling to find management," JC recalled in an interview with *Teen Beat* magazine. "Every day was a four hour routine. Joey would get off from work at nine o'clock at night and we'd go into this warehouse and we'd rehearse from like nine to one, straight dancing and singing all night. Plus, during the day, in between times, we'd be doing just vocal rehearsals. We'd be working at least five hours a day working on our trade, plus these guys were working full time at Universal and they were going to school. But we knew what we wanted to do and we concentrated on it. Whenever we had free time, that's when we put our energy into it."

"It really exhausts you when you jump around four times a week for three to five hours in 90-degree heat," Justin told *16* magazine. "But we didn't really think of it as a sacrifice. We love to do what we're doing right now, so we all had to make sacrifices, but to us they were small sacrifices compared to what we've gotten to do." This attitude kept the quartet working, and within just a few months, they clicked. The harmonies sounded smooth and the dances were in step. They knew they had something special.

The Wright Stuff

"We did a demo package on our own at Pleasure Island. We videotaped the whole thing and we created a package," JC told *All-Stars* magazine. "We sang some stuff in the studio, put it on a CD, and sent it out to all these different record companies. It came across the desk of our manager and he was interested in it. So, Johnny Wright picked us up and then he shopped for our deal." Wait a minute. Back up a few words. Did you say Johnny Wright?!

It's easy for JC to casually drop the name now that he's a huge success, but, at the time, 'N Sync finding out they got "picked up by Johnny Wright" was the equivalent of you saying, "Oh, yeah, Leonardo DiCaprio gave me a call last night. He mentioned something about getting together this weekend."

Johnny Wright is one of the most well known managers in the record industry. He played a major role in launching the Backstreet Boys as well as the fabled New Kids on the Block. By the way, by "picked up" JC means Johnny Wright became their manager. In case you're wondering, this indeed was 'N Sync's big break.

Wright knows all the important players in the record industry worldwide, and they all know him. Wright signed the group to Lou Pearlman's small Orlando-based record label, Trans Continental Entertainment, and then began sending the group's demo package out to record companies in search of a recording contract. Meanwhile, he hooked the guys up with world famous choreographer Robert Jacquez, who'd previously worked with Janet Jackson, Prince, and Michael Jackson.

With Jacquez's tutelage, the quartet's dancing vastly improved, and with further studio work with a vocal coach, their harmonies continued to sharpen as well. Their sound was crisp and clean, but something was missing. The vocal coach knew it, Wright knew it, and so did the guys. "Even when we signed the first time, we knew we weren't complete yet," Chris said in an interview with *16* magazine. "We knew we needed a bass to round off our sound. So, it was just a matter of getting our name on a contract. We were only going to be satisfied when he [Wright] signed the bass."

The Missing Puzzle Piece

"We called our vocal coach and he recommended Lance," Joey added. Lance, of course, is Mississippi-born Lance Bass, who had worked with the same coach himself while singing in high school. Lance had just the booming, deep voice the group needed to complement Chris's soprano voice and the alto sounds of JC, Joey, and Justin. "When we got Lance, we were so eager to sing together," Chris told *Tiger Beat* magazine. "Actually, we'd signed with a smaller record label a few months before but we didn't even know Lance because four of us signed as a group. I think we did more celebrating after we signed Lance and did our first couple of shows together."

Lance proved to be the missing piece to the puzzle as the group's manager was suddenly fielding offers from record companies. Meanwhile, the group continued to practice with all their might, only now they'd do it as a quintet. "We worked all the beginning of '96, just rehearsing every day, and then, in the summer of '96, that's when we got our deal," JC fondly recalled in *Teen Machine* magazine.

The "deal" was a certified recording contract with BMG Ariola Munich, the world headquarters of one of the six largest conglomerate record companies in the world. Suddenly, a lifelong dream had come true for five hardworking young men. But, there was no time for celebrating, Justin told *All-Stars* magazine. "Two days after we signed the contracts, they said, 'Pack your stuff, we're leaving.'" "And we haven't stopped since," Lance added.

Getting On Like Brothers

There were a number of amazing things about how JC, Justin, Chris, Joey, and Lance came together, like how well their voices blended and how they all shared the same ambitions. But what made it truly seem like their union was driven by fate is the fact that they all get along like brothers. "The five of us are like family and we all look out for each other," Justin said in *TV Hits* magazine.

Even during down time the guys opt to hang out together, playing basketball, going to the beach, and going out dancing. Without question, the chemistry between the guys shows onstage during performances, as they constantly play off of one another vocally and visually during concerts. The five also respect each other from a professional standpoint. "As far as making decisions, it's a democracy," Justin explained to *Tiger Beat* magazine. "It's good because we have an odd amount of people so it divides things up three to two."

Surely, considering how much time they spend together, the guys must have their share of disagreements. "We fight about stupid stuff," Chris admitted on The Disney Channel. "I was playing this video game first!" Justin added. "I was here first! Stop touching me! Will you stop touching me!" Joey said jokingly.

So, now that everything was in place, all this band needed was a name. "Actually, my mom came up with the name," Justin told *Teen Beat* magazine. "We shot it around and thought it was a good name to represent us. Shortly after we copyrighted it, we recognized that all the last letters of our names spelled 'N Sync."

Joey went on to clarify, "When we first met Lance, we called him 'Lansten' as a nickname. So, it worked—Justin for the N, Chris for the S,

Joey for the Y, Lansten for the N, and JC for the C."

"We didn't plan for it to end up as a promotional gimmick," Justin explained. "I want everyone to know that. We just thought it was a funny fact for ourselves."

"The name explains the band," Chris told *Smash Hits* magazine. "Although we're all very different people, our voices and personalities work well together." Thank goodness for that, because the five guys would be spending an absurd amount of time together, working their tails off to launch their band over the next two years.

2

here we go!

With no time to celebrate their good fortune or, for that matter, even let the news sink in, JC, Justin, Chris, Joey, and Lance packed their belongings and headed for Europe. "We went to Munich, Germany [where BMG is headquartered], for a year and a half," Joey explained in *Superstars* magazine.

Once settled in Germany, Wright and BMG executives worked their magic and 'N Sync got hooked up with a battery of talented producers, arrangers, and songwriters, including Kristian Lundin, Veit Renn, Christian Hamm, Gary Carolla, and Full Force. Wright served as the Executive Producer on the album. "We recorded the album in Germany and we recorded our first hit in Sweden," Justin told *Teen Machine* magazine.

Singin' in Sweden

That first hit, "I Want You Back," as well as their second single, "Tearin' Up My Heart," were recorded at Cheiron Studios in Stockholm, Sweden, where 'N Sync met up with renowned songwriter Max Martin and dance producer Denniz Pop. Martin and Pop had dozens of hit songs to their credit, including several by the Backstreet Boys, Robyn, Ace of Base, and 3T. When the dynamic duo got together in the recording studio with 'N Sync, the results were sensational.

"We thought it was something cool, because we think our voices have more of an R&B feel," JC commented in *All-Stars* magazine. "But when you mix it with that dance beat you put under it, it's something really different, and you get so many cool things, like the harmonies and the little riffs and things. It's like a mix between a break beat and a hip-hop feel, and it's something you can really dance to."

European music listeners sure felt the same way, because in no time, both singles raced up the pop charts, breaking the Top 10 in several countries. "I Want You Back" set records in Germany, reaching the Top 10 in record time and remaining there for eight weeks straight. The last time such numbers were reached in Germany was over fifteen years ago when the country was introduced to Michael Jackson's *Thriller*, which went on to become one of the top selling albums of all time.

"We were all very excited for it to be happening so fast but we weren't exactly ready," Chris recalled in *Billboard* magazine. "We had to put the album together in about two or three months, sometimes recording a song a day, and started radio promotion like crazy." But, all the blood, sweat, and tears 'N Sync put into the recording paid off because, in 1997, when their self-titled debut album was released in Europe, it hit gold all over the continent and reached number one in Germany. The 14-track CD got a substantial international fan base hooked on the infectious grooves of the American pop quintet.

After promoting their debut album in Germany, Austria, and Switzerland through a series of appearances and mini-concerts, 'N

Sync developed a following so huge they were no longer able to walk the streets without hordes of screaming fans running after them. "We usually have to take two or three bodyguards with us there," Justin said in *Billboard* magazine.

Worldwide Wonder

"We've had such big success in Europe because we went there first with BMG Europe," Chris told *Tiger Beat* magazine. "We signed just this last February ['98] to RCA [major American record label owned by parent company BMG] here in the U.S." 'N Sync mania didn't happen in Europe first by accident. Manager Johnny Wright knew that a few years ago, the American market was not as responsive to pop music as Europe was. For whatever reason, the resurgence of pop happened in Europe first. Wright knew this well from his experience with the Backstreet Boys, who flopped on their first crack at the United States in 1995 but flourished their second time around in 1998, after they'd established themselves overseas.

Joey understands the theory well and explained it in *Superstars* magazine. "Europe is where pop music was at the time, and that's why it wasn't time to come here. If we would have come out a year earlier, people would have said, 'That's silly.' It wasn't the right time, but groups like the Spice Girls broke open doors."

In an otherwise unrelated story, it was around this time that 'N Sync encountered the Spice Girls in an airport in Germany. "They didn't have security and we didn't have security," Chris recalled during an interview with *16* magazine. "We met them in the airport and we just sat down and talked with them. People were walking right by us."

"We recognized them from the video," JC added. "We recognized Scary Spice's hair. They were still so new with it, like us. We told them, 'We're going to record a really cool song!'"

Airports became quite commonplace to 'N Sync as they spent the remainder of the year buzzing around the globe, introducing the rest of the world to their new record. First stop—London. Already in love with the Backstreet Boys, Boyzone, and the Spice Girls, Great Britain had plenty of room for another pop group. 'N Sync quickly became the darlings of the British press, doing photo shoots and interviews with all the music magazines, fanzines and pop radio stations, all the while charming the pants off of interviewers and photographers as well as the legions of loyal readers and viewers. By the time they left Great Britain, 'N Sync was on the pop charts and a number of magazine covers, as well as on the minds of thousands of young British girls.

Following their very successful stay in England, the guys spent the last few months of 1997 promoting *'N Sync* in Asia, South Africa, and Mexico before finally returning home to Orlando. Launching abroad before doing it at home afforded 'N Sync a chance to catch their breath. "We consider it lucky that we hit in Europe and got so huge but remained unknown in the States," Justin added. "It gave us the chance to sit back and digest what was happening as it happened." Indeed it kept the guys' egos firmly in check. "We might have gotten crazy about it, but then we'd come home and it was like a reality check," Justin said in *Billboard* magazine.

What a long strange trip it had been! "We certainly didn't expect things to go as well as they did in Europe," Justin told *Billboard* magazine. "We hope to have half as much success in the U.S."

Bringin' It Home

Within days after the start of 1998, an RCA press release was sent out to all entertainment media in the U.S. The release detailed the success 'N Sync had enjoyed overseas and prepared magazine writers and news reporters for the introduction of the next great pop band in America. Ready or not, here they come!

JC, Justin, Lance, Chris, and Joey were immediately thrown right into the fire of an all-out media blitz. Over the next three months, 'N Sync would tackle a flurry of magazine interviews, photo shoots, and television and radio appearances. They took on pop radio stations, news programs, networks, and newspapers. The band visited MTV, VH1, and Much Music. They met with reporters at all the major music and entertainment magazines, like *Billboard* and *Entertainment Weekly*. And they clobbered the teen press, both the senior circuit—*Seventeen, YM, Teen,* and *Teen People*—and the junior circuit—*Teen Beat, 16, Twist, Bop, Tiger Beat,* and many others.

All the while, RCA was working overtime to get the group's first single, "I Want You Back," on the radio, its accompanying video on the cable networks, and the debut CD, *'N Sync,* in record stores. "I Want You Back" was added to Top 40 radio station play lists across America in January and made the regular rotations of sixty major stations in the first week. By the time the single became available commercially in February, it was being played on hundreds of radio stations of all different formats, including rhythm, dance, and Top 40.

"The reason we're excited to release the single here in the U.S. is it's a little bit different from what you usually hear in pop," JC said in an early interview with *16* magazine. "A lot of things that have been released that weren't rocked out were ballads."

Hi, We're 'N Sync

The "I Want You Back" video became an instant staple on all the music video channels, and by the time their self-titled debut was released on March 24, everybody knew who 'N Sync was. The video did more than help promote the song—it introduced Justin, JC, Joey, Lance, and Chris to America. The half black-and-white, half color video didn't just capture the feel of the song, it captured the essence of the boys of 'N Sync. Watching the video gave you a sense of the group's camaraderie, as well as their looks, styles, and playfulness.

The "I Want You Back" video is who they are. Justin and Chris play a competitive but friendly game of one-on-one basketball that ends in a silly water fight. Joey goes out to clubs and shoots pool and then goes Jet Skiing with

Lance before shoving him into the water. Meanwhile JC drives around in a convertible in pursuit of "the girl."

If you look deeper into the video, you'll realize JC is doing more than driving. He's behind the wheel and in control while the other guys are in the passenger and back seats. This is not to say he's the leader of 'N Sync, because he'd be the first to remind you that he's not, but it does point out that he is a pillar of responsibility and a guiding force for the other band members. The video also shows that when the guys are all done doing their thing on their own, they always come back to each other. And when JC's heart gets broken he turns to his band mates.

In a matter of four minutes, you know who the guys of 'N Sync are and you're also hooked on the pop-soul sound of "I Want You Back." You want more. The single had the same effect on the radio, leading to caller requests and letters to the stations. By the time the album came out in March, "I Want You Back" had broken the *Billboard* Hot 100 Singles chart. Incredibly, it would stay there right through the end of summer, for a sensational six months, peaking at number 13, and going gold in the process.

"When we first heard this song, with its groove, and the heavy beat behind it, we knew it was a hit," JC told *Teen People* magazine.

With all the excitement over "I Want You Back," Lance couldn't believe his ears. "I heard the song on the radio on *Casey's Top 40,* and it was weird, because we all grew up listening to Casey Kasem. It sounded so good!" he gushed.

"That song's our baby," Chris said in *Superstars* magazine. "We broke three different records with it in Europe," Lance added. And Americans didn't seem to mind it either.

3

'N-Sanity

That the American public was falling 'n love with 'N Sync was great news. The bad news is that meant there was no stopping the express train of promotion, publicity, and performance that the band was riding. As busy as 'N Sync was with publicity in the winter, they'd be equally busy with promotion in the spring and summer.

April Wowers

Following the release of their debut album at the end of March, 'N Sync spent the month of April promoting it by paying many visits to radio stations and record stores. That month, the fab five flew back and forth between Los Angeles, New York, and Orlando enough times to earn their wings. They dropped by dozens of major record store chains, like Tower Records and Sam

Goody, to meet and greet fans while autographing just-bought copies of their new CD. They stopped by station after station, where they would do on-air interviews, answer fan questions, and, of course, plug their debut album.

By the end of April, thousands of fans had gotten an up close and personal impression of America's newest heartthrob band. Justin, JC, Joey, Lance, and Chris were all exhausted, but that never stopped them before, so they kept on movin'.

Madness in May

In the month of May, 'N Sync spent time in Minneapolis, Orlando, and New York City, and made three landmark performances in the process. Minneapolis was the first major stop, and 'N Sync created quite a stir when they played a free concert outside the Mall of America in nearby Bloomington. Even the largest mall in North America couldn't contain the excitement as thousands of young fans filled the parking lot to see 'N Sync play a live set.

"It was so funny because we were getting ready for the show under the lower level and we couldn't hear anything," Justin recalled in *16* magazine. "We walked up and there was a line that security made going to the stage. There were about two or three hundred people and we saw people blocked into this section, and we found out later that there were six or seven thousand people. We were like, 'wow!' We came on stage and it was just, raaah [crowd sounds]!"

With the Midwest quivering in the wake of 'N Sync mayhem, the boys were off to their hometown of Orlando. But there would be little time for family fun as they were to be part of a weekend-long Walt Disney World event. The purpose of the event was twofold: to promote Disney World's newest theme park addition, Animal Kingdom, and for 'N Sync to perform for The Disney Channel's new *In Concert* series. Although the five boys were constantly the center of attention during the long and very hot weekend, they were good sports about it, and even managed to have a little fun themselves.

Disney Days

On Friday of that weekend, 'N Sync got a private tour of the Animal Kingdom. A Disney camera crew followed them around as they checked out the wildlife and watched demonstrations. The guys had a blast during the tour. They commented on odd-looking animals, imitated bird sounds, and, of course, teased one another along the way. Afterward they granted interviews to magazine press at the Rainforest Cafe.

When asked about their grueling schedule, Joey answered, "We've actually just had a little bit of a break and now we're starting to get back into things with all the promotion. We're doing this special, we're doing a show in New York soon . . ."

". . . and we've been doing a lot of radio shows," Lance added. "In Anaheim, we did six thousand people!"

The next night, 'N Sync would perform a live show in front of a crowd of thousands that would later be telecast for millions to see. "We're very excited about it," Lance said.

"We've been rehearsing for like a week now with a live band," JC enthused. At the conclusion of the interview, four out of five 'N Sync members expressed their eagerness by bursting into an impromptu a cappella version of "I Drive Myself Crazy." Chris refrained because he was nursing a sore throat.

Afterward, 'N Sync was interviewed by The Disney Channel. When the guys were all talked out, they got to spend the remainder of the day enjoying the rest of the rides and attractions in the Animal Kingdom. With many of their family members in tow, JC, Justin, Lance, Chris, and Joey went on the Safari Ride, a monorail, the Extinction Ride, and visited the Tree of Life. By the end of the day the guys were wiped out and headed back to their hotel for some much needed rest. After all, they had a big day ahead of them.

'N Sync got the full star treatment on Saturday morning. First they took part in a handprint ceremony where they had cement moldings of their hands made on the sidewalk outside a replica of Mann's Chinese Theater, in Hollywood,

California. The ten handprints (two for each guy) took their rightful place next to those of many other celebrities, including Harrison Ford, Bette Midler, and Robin Williams. Afterwards, three thousand fans were invited to the *Beauty & The Beast* Amphitheater for an interactive Q&A session with 'N Sync. On the way there, the guys drove through a parade of confetti in two vintage convertibles with Mickey and Minnie Mouse in tow.

After a Disney Channel moderator asked the guys a series of questions about how they met and got started as a band, the mike was turned over to the anxious crowd. The young crowd surprisingly fired off some hard-hitting questions, ranging from "Do you do your own choreography?" to "What do your parents think about the group?" Of course, a few simple ones were thrown in too, like "What cars do you drive?" and "Are any of you single?"

One particularly bold fan raised her hand and said, "Today's my friend's birthday. Can you sing 'Happy Birthday' to her?" Without batting an eye, the guys belted out a harmonious rendition of "Happy Birthday to Kayla." Chris jokingly added, "That will be twenty-five dollars."

When the crowd Q&A was completed, 'N Sync went backstage for more interviews, this time with local newspapers. Following a few hours of rehearsal, vocal warm-ups, and sound checks, it was time to take to the stage. Fans in attendance were treated to a memorable performance that included covers of songs by the Bee Gees and Michael Jackson, as well as plenty of 'N Sync favorites from their debut album, and even a stunning offering of "The Lion Sleeps Tonight." A rousing performance of "Tearin' Up My Heart" was highlighted by an over-the-top acrobatic dance act that included an in sync back flip by JC, Justin, and Joey.

The show, which featured tons of choreographed dancing, props, wardrobe changes, and a crowd sing-along, left the audience screaming for more. And they would get it two months later when the concert and previous interview footage would air on The Disney Channel as *'N Sync In Concert.* Though their *In Concert* special followed in the footsteps of

LeAnn Rimes, Jonny Lang, and Brandy, 'N Sync's special got by far the highest ratings of any special in the series. Due to viewer demand, it was subsequently aired an additional six times over the summer. RCA Records credits the Disney special for driving sales of 'N Sync's debut album. The fans on hand weren't just a part of a special performance, they were part of music history.

Jumpin' June

After their whirlwind weekend at Disney World, 'N Sync flew up to New York City for Z-Day, a star-studded benefit concert put on by Top 40 radio station Z-100. The show was held at the world-famous Radio City Music Hall and celebrated New York's one hundredth anniversary while it raised money for PAX, a nonprofit organization dedicated to ending gun violence. The audience of thousands was blown away by spectacular performances from Mariah Carey, Gloria Estefan, Olivia Newton-John, K-Ci & JoJo, Third Eye Blind, Paula Cole, Matchbox

20, and, of course, 'N Sync, who brought the house down when they hopped onstage.

According to a review in *Billboard* magazine, "Among favorite moments for the sold-out Radio City Music Hall crowd [was] . . . a performance by 'N Sync, who danced and sang like banshees amid throngs of mesmerized and screaming girls."

"That was so cool!" Joey gushed in *All-Stars* magazine. "I mean, when do you really get to play at Radio City?!"

Sizzlin' Summer

There was no slowing down 'N Sync as they trekked across North America, winning over new fans at every stop. A series of radio promotion mini-concerts had the five guys spending days in every nook and cranny of the United States. 'N Sync headed north of the border and did the same in Canada, spending most of July bouncing back and forth between Vancouver and Toronto, with plenty of stops in between.

The heat wave continued well into August

when 'N Sync returned to the U.S. "We did a theme park tour in August, you know Six Flags and state fairs," Lance told a Disney Channel correspondent.

"We've been doing mall shows. We hooked up with *YM* [magazine] and the cosmetic Fetish," Justin said.

"We don't use it though," Joey pointed out. "Yeah, it smells pretty girly," Justin added with a giggle.

In addition to the mall appearances, 'N Sync also showed their adorable mugs on a couple of talk shows, landing on *Live! with Regis & Kathie Lee* and *The Tonight Show with Jay Leno.* With success in hand and fame on their side, 'N Sync began thinking it was time to give something back and got involved with two more charity events in August. "I think you just do as much as you can," Chris told a *Teen Beat* magazine reporter. "When I was little, I tried to do as much as I could as often as I could. Now that we've got a name out there, it's a lot easier for us to do more for charity because you can appeal to the masses."

The first good cause 'N Sync lent a hand

to was SWAT—Students Working Against Tobacco—a youth organization committed to fighting teen smoking by taking on Hollywood and the media. SWAT organized a mega-event in Florida called The Truth Train, a huge statewide awareness program that was highlighted by outdoor concerts by more than fifteen bands. Although several big-name bands and musicians, such as Montell Jordan, LFO, Liquid Vinyl, and Big Sky, performed, when it came time for the final encore on the last day of The Truth Train event in Palm Beach, 'N Sync was given the honor. Now that's a sign that they had definitely arrived.

Before they could catch their breath from the anti-smoking event, 'N Sync was on a plane again, this time headed for Los Angeles for the KIIS-FM Wango Tango benefit. The annual event, sponsored by the L.A. area Top 40 radio station, featured outdoor concerts as part of a fund-raiser for local charities. "Today was dope! We had a lot of fun," JC enthused to a *Teen Beat* reporter on hand for the huge event. "We played in a stadium and it was a huge rush to be on that stage in front of that many people. There was a good vibe because it was for a good cause too, so we enjoyed it."

JC and his band mates truly have hearts of gold. In fact, 'N Sync also found time last summer to pitch in for an on-line fund-raiser for a National Institutes of Health charity called "Kids to Kids." After the Wango Tango event, JC and Chris talked with *All-Stars* magazine about the importance of charity involvement. "Well, [charity work] is always gonna be around you, you just have to take the initiative and look for it for yourself," JC said. "You have to be the one who wants to be involved. Hopefully, there's some good-hearted kids who want to help other people."

Meanwhile, Chris continued to gush about the day's giant arena performance. "It was a lot of fun and it was for a good cause," Chris said. "We were really tired. We just did a show last night in Orlando and we had to fly here at like four this morning, so we were beat when we got off the plane. But, you know, when it's for a good cause and the crowd gets you hyped up it always makes it so much easier." Easier said than done, Chris.

'N Sync's next appearance was a bit more lighthearted. They performed on national television for the Miss Teen USA Pageant. After that, the guys headed back to New York (again) for an event that would put a giant exclamation point on their nonstop summer.

'N Sync Takes Manhattan

When international entertainment mogul Richard Branson prepared for the grand opening of his brand-new downtown New York City Virgin Mega Store, he pulled out all the stops. So that everyone east of the Mississippi River would know about his giant new record store, Branson enlisted the help of dozens of celebrities, including our boys, 'N Sync.

The daylong event began with 'N Sync riding on top of a double-decker tour bus with Branson, singer Petula Clark, and camera crews from *CNN Headline News* and *Entertainment Tonight.* The bus began its inter-city route at the

Virgin Mega Store's uptown location in Times Square in midtown Manhattan (also where 'N Sync's label, RCA Records, is located). The entourage-topped bus headed downtown and made several stops, at the New York Public Library and in Greenwich Village, before reaching the grand-opening site in downtown Union Square. Along the way, 'N Sync and Petula Clark waved to crowds of onlookers, sang, and granted interviews at the stops, while the bus caused several downtown traffic jams. "I'm used to riding on a bus, just not one without a top," Justin told one reporter on board with him.

When 'N Sync and company reached the new store, they circled the block several times before stopping in front, on the corner of Broadway and 14th Street, where they were greeted by a scene that included barricades, police officers on horseback, and several hundred screaming girls. Without a moment's hesitation, 'N Sync grabbed their microphones and sang "I Want You Back" for the delighted young fans, who sang the words right back to them, "You're all I ever wanted. You're all I ever needed . . ."

Justin, JC, Lance, Chris, and Joey then hopped off the bus and were escorted by police and bodyguards through the sea of waving hands, bouncing feet, and high-pitched shrieks into the store. For over an hour the guys sat at a table in the entrance to the store signing autographs and shaking hands with lucky fans who had waited a long time for that moment.

Suddenly September

'N Sync spent the last week of summer on a Macy's tour, performing daytime concerts outside the department stores in New York, Atlanta, and Boston. Things got sweeter in September as 'N Sync got involved in a promotion with Twix chocolate candy that made a select bunch of their fans among the luckiest people alive. To kick off their "Double or Nothing" instant win game, M&M/Mars, the company that makes Twix, threw a huge bash at New York City's Twin Towers (get it?), at which contest winners got to meet 'N Sync. *Rolling Stone* magazine was on hand, both as a co-sponsor of the event, and to cover the festivities for an upcoming feature.

Through a Z-100 FM radio contest, one hundred on-line trivia contest winners and a guest were invited to the exclusive Rock the Towers music party at Windows on the World, the famous restaurant atop the World Trade Center. Half of those winners were then serenaded by 'N Sync in a private concert. Afterward, they were lucky enough to meet the band and then ask them questions in an intimate Q&A session. Several of the contest winners nearly lost control of themselves, while others got choked up and were too nervous to ask any questions. Nonetheless, they all left with quite a story to tell their friends!

'N Sync did find time to have some fun in September when they participated in MTV's *Rock 'N Jock Presents: The Game.* Justin, JC, Lance, Chris, and Joey got to show off their basketball skills in a celebrity game that featured NBA stars as well as musicians and actors. They also demonstrated their fashion sense by sporting matching light blue 'N Sync basketball jerseys.

4

dazzling debut

"We collaborate on everything," Justin told *Teen Beat* magazine. "I think we have our influence on everything we do, not just the dancing, but also on the music. If we don't like the song, our producers won't make us do it. We've had chances to come up with our own harmonies, and things like that." That's proof positive that despite all the producers, songwriters, and arrangers who helped create 'N Sync, at the bottom of it all, it was the talent, resolve, and hard work of the five guys in the band that made it a smash.

'N Sync

In early March, a few weeks before 'N Sync's 13-track, self-titled American debut was released, radio stations and music writers were sent advance copies for review purposes.

Everyone, from *Billboard* to the daily newspapers to the teen press, agreed; it was a solid album full of fluid harmonies, lingering melodies, and upbeat rhythms that make you want to get up and dance.

A few critics said 'N Sync sounded too much like other pop bands, specifically the Backstreet Boys, but that didn't discourage the guys one bit. "It's like when Toni Braxton came out," JC pointed out in the *New York Post*. "Everyone compared her to Whitney Houston and Mariah Carey. But, if you have talent, you'll stand out." Music fans agreed, because from the minute *'N Sync* landed on record store shelves, copies were flying out the door.

'N Sync hit the *Billboard* 200 album chart almost instantly and stayed there (thirty-five weeks at last check). Thousands more young music fans were turned on to the magic of 'N Sync in July when the *'N Sync In Concert* Disney Channel special aired. The highly rated special spurred those thousands to buy *'N Sync*, driving the album to platinum status (over a million copies sold in America).

In the summer of 1998, when "Tearin' Up My Heart" was released for radio play, it quickly became a hit and further pushed album sales to the point where *'N Sync* surpassed albums from pop mainstays like the Backstreet Boys, Spice Girls, and Matchbox 20. By mid-September, the album was at number three and had achieved double-platinum status.

The "Tearin' Up My Heart" video introduced fans to another side of 'N Sync, the light-footed, high steppin', back flippin' side. The contagious dance floor pulse of the single, coupled with the high-energy dancing in the video, made it a surefire hit. (And it didn't hurt the group's chances that the video turned young Justin Timberlake into a heartthrob either!)

With "Tearin' Up My Heart" tearin' up the charts, and a third single, "God Must Have Spent a Little More Time on You," on the way, a number one album was well within reach for 'N Sync. And with a major American tour and a number of TV specials upcoming, the fresh-faced five would no doubt reach triple-platinum status with their very first album.

Background Check

Although the debut album that 'N Sync released in America shared the same eponymous name and the same first two singles as their European debut, they were not exactly the same record. The European version did not contain the songs "I Just Wanna Be with You," "God Must Have Spent a Little More Time on You," "Everything I Own," and "I Drive Myself Crazy," and in their place had the following tracks: "Riddle," "Best of My Life," "More Than a Feeling," "Together Again," and "Forever Young." (If you *must* have both versions of 'N Sync, check the import section of your local record store. If they don't have it on hand, they may be able to special order it for you, but it will cost a bit more.)

Here is a breakdown of all of the songs on both albums, complete with background information, studio talk, and behind-the-scenes players who were involved. (Songs marked with an asterisk appear on both versions of the album.)

"Tearin' Up My Heart"

Famed songwriters Kristian Lundin (Ace of

Base and Robyn) and Max Martin (Backstreet Boys, 5ive) wrote and produced "Tearin' Up My Heart" at the Cheiron Studio in Stockholm, Sweden, and the 'N Sync boys fell in love with it. The lyrics are about a strained relationship in which the girl is sending mixed signals and the guy is confused about what she wants.

The unstoppable beat of "Tearin' Up My Heart" is enough to bounce a wallflower out of his or her seat and onto the dance floor. Meanwhile, the melody stays in your head long after the song is over, making you want to play it over and over. It's truly an addictive song and a logical choice for 'N Sync's second single release.

"I Just Wanna Be with You"

"I Just Wanna Be with You" features the ingenious work of legendary producers Full Force, who wrote, produced, and arranged the song. The R&B side of 'N Sync comes out in this song. The track was mixed and recorded at three different studios and features sampling from the classic hit "Family Affair."

*"Here We Go"

This bouncy party hook is an 'N Sync favorite for concerts. The band often uses this upbeat little ditty to get the crowd fired up and singing along with them. "Here We Go" was co-written and co-produced by B. Aris, T. Cottura, and V. D. Toorn for BOOYA Music Productions.

*"For the Girl Who Has Everything"

Veit Renn teamed up with Jolyon Skinner to make "For the Girl Who Has Everything" possible. Skinner co-wrote and played bass guitar for the song, while Renn co-wrote, produced, and played electric guitar. The theme of this song is almost *Titanic*-esque, with a young guy pleading for a chance with a beautiful rich girl. "For the Girl Who Has Everything" is a smooth ballad that allows all five guys to display their crystal clear voices.

"God Must Have Spent a Little More Time on You"

A tremendous amount of work went into this song, which was recorded and arranged in three different studios and features a background of acoustic guitar, violins, and cellos. The vocals in the song have a very soothing feel to them. "God Must Have Spent a Little More Time on You" is the longest song on the album and served as the third single in the U.S.

"You Got It"

The Romeo in each 'N Sync boy comes out whenever they sing this song about a guy trying to convince a girl to go out with him by telling her how romantic he can be. "You Got It" is backed by an infectious urban dance beat that blends well with 'N Sync's singing. Veit Renn wrote and produced the song for 'N Sync, who recorded it in Orlando, Florida.

"I Need Love"

Written and produced by Gary Carolla, this may be 'N Sync's most sentimental song. "I Need Love" is a simple love song for the romantic in all of us. However, the fast-paced electronic backing gives it the energetic rhythm of a No Mercy song.

"I Want You Back"

"The song is about suddenly finding yourself separated from the person you feel so deeply about because you've done something stupid to screw it up," JC explained in *Teen People* magazine. "I think it hits people because they can relate to it like a love song, but it's powerful and up-tempo enough to kick them too."

"I Want You Back" was recorded in Stockholm, Sweden, with the help of Denniz Pop, the late dance track master, and songwriter Max Martin ("Everybody [Backstreet's Back]"). The catchy, upbeat song made the perfect first single for 'N Sync.

"Everything I Own"

Folk-rock group Bread put this song, originally written by David Gates, on the radio back in the 1970s, and 'N Sync did quite a rendition of it on their debut CD. If you want to know what sets 'N Sync apart from other boy bands, listen to this song. The tenderness of five fluid vocals blend together beautifully in this cover of "Everything I Own." With the help of Full

Force, who provided production, arrangement, and additional performance, 'N Sync turned this tune into a very different song, in a good way.

"I Drive Myself Crazy"

Recently released as a single in Germany, this song has a bit of an edge to it. The whisper-to-a-scream track begins with a gentle acoustic guitar and Chris's soprano pipes, and moves to a hard guitar, thumping bass, and the alternating voices of the other four guys in the band. Originally written by Ellen Shipley, "I Drive Myself Crazy" was produced for 'N Sync by Veit Renn. Tony Battaglia provides the smokin' guitar riffs.

*"Crazy for You"

This adorable track about love from afar was co-written for 'N Sync by Alain Bertoni and Christian Hamm, who also served as composer. With a thumping bass beat, mixed instrumentals, and varying paces, "Crazy for You" is almost like several songs in one, and they're all good. Gary Carolla produced and mixed the song in Orlando. Mark Matteo plays guitar.

*"Sailing"

Singer/songwriter Christopher Cross made this tender ballad a hit in 1980, and 'N Sync made it just as sweet with their own version. Veit Renn served as producer. "I always heard this song growing up," JC said in the *New York Post.* "It was my father's favorite song." The way JC delivers this song, it makes you think what a great solo artist he could be (if he didn't love his band mates so much, that is).

*"Giddy Up"

'N Sync and Veit Renn co-wrote this song about reconciling a romance. "Giddy Up" has more of an urban feel than any other 'N Sync song and the result is funky fun. Renn also produced the song and provided the guitar playing. "Giddy Up" was mixed in Orlando.

The following songs only appeared in the European version

"Riddle"

"Riddle" is a funny little song about boys trying to figure out what makes a girl tick, specifically, the one they have a crush on. "Riddle" was written by Pat Reiniz, produced by Veit Renn in Europe, and later mixed by Joe Smith in Florida.

"Best of My Life"

The title of this song is rather ironic considering it's actually about a painful breakup. "Best of My Life" was co-written and co-produced by B. Aris, T. Cottura, and V. D. Toorn for BOOYA Music Productions.

"More Than a Feeling"

"More Than a Feeling" was originally made into a hard rock hit by Boston in the 1970s. 'N Sync put their own spin on the simple tune about being equally passionate about music and love. Originally written by T. Scholz, the cover song was produced in Holland by Jaap Eggermont.

"Together Again"

Co-written by Andy Reynolds and Tee Green, "Together Again" is a song about the complications and heartache of long-distance romance. Gary Carolla and Veit Renn produced the song in Europe, but the finishing touches were put on it in Florida.

"Forever Young"

This song is very personal to JC, Justin, Joey, Lance, and Chris because it is about their early days, recalling their hard work, patience, and optimism in the face of adversity. "Forever Young" was written and composed by Nemo Frankenkrog-Peterson and co-written by Jean Beauvoir and Bettina Martinelli. It was produced by Joern-Uwe Frankenkrog-Peterson and Frank Busch in Berlin, Germany.

5

justin

With his heart-melting blue eyes and baby-cute smile, it's no wonder Justin Timberlake, the youngest member of 'N Sync at just seventeen, has become a monthly pinup in every teen magazine from *TV Hits* in Australia to *Teen Beat* in America to *Smash Hits* in Great Britain. The Tennessee native is still getting used to all the attention he gets. "I don't know what to say to that," he told *16* magazine.

Despite his amazement, Justin's rise to fame was more gradual than it was for some of his band mates. Having begun his career as a professional musician at a younger age and with two years of the *Mickey Mouse Club* under his belt, Justin has eased into the driver's seat of the 'N Sync fame mobile. But the fact remains that in just seventeen short years, Justin has gone from playful tot to musical youth to TV star to one of the most recognizable faces in the world

Tennessee Tot

On January 31, 1981, Randy and Lynn Timberlake welcomed an angelic baby boy into the world and christened him Justin Randall Timberlake. The curly blond–haired, blue-eyed boy was brought back to his home in Memphis, Tennessee, where his proud parents showed him off to family, friends, and neighbors. From the time he was just a tot, Justin made it obvious that he liked being the center of attention.

Justin's parents divorced when he was young, and both have since remarried. While Justin still maintains a relationship with his birth father, Randy, and Randy's wife, Lisa, he was raised mostly by his mother, Lynn, and stepfather, Paul Harless. Despite the divorce, it was a happy childhood for Justin, who grew up with a big family and lots of pets, including two dogs, Scooter and Ozzie (who he still owns), and two cats, Millie and Alley. The support of two sets of loving parents and four sets of doting grandparents made childhood all the more pleasant for Justin. In the liner notes for 'N Sync's European-released debut album, Justin thanked "my beloved parents for teaching me what love means, and also, for letting me live my dreams. [and] My grandparents (all of you!) for spoiling me rotten!"

Justin now has two half brothers, four-year-old Jonathan, whom he collects tour souvenirs for, and baby Steven. "Yes, I have a new half-brother," Justin bragged to *16* magazine. "He was born on August fourteenth [1998] and I got word from my daddy that he looks exactly like my one-month-old pictures. He's got to be a hideous little lizard," he joked. In all likelihood, he's so cute you'd want to pinch his cheeks, which brings us back to young Justin.

At the age of eight, Justin's parents found an outlet for his energy and hidden talents. "I grew up singing in church," Justin told *Teen Beat* magazine. "Then I got into voice lessons when I was about eight. Then I did talent shows and things, and from that moment on, I knew that's what I wanted to do." Among those talent shows was a stage performance at the Grand Ole Opry and an appearance on the long-running TV talent showcase *Star Search.* At this point, Justin's life would begin to change quickly, both personally and professionally.

The Speed of Life

Justin was eleven when he made his appearance as a junior vocalist on *Star Search*. This gave him the opportunity to show off his singing and dancing talents to millions of television viewers, at least one of which turned out to be an entertainment industry executive. A casting director approached Justin and his mom with the offer to join the cast of The Disney Channel's long-running franchise *The Mickey Mouse Club*. With that, Justin and his folks packed their things and moved to Orlando, Florida, where the show is taped.

Being uprooted from his neighborhood, friends, and school back in Tennessee wasn't easy for Justin, but it didn't take long for his outgoing personality to attract more friends than he'd ever had. Between going to school, playing basketball, and being a part of *The Mickey Mouse Club*, Justin had countless opportunities to meet new people his age. (In fact, in sixth grade, as Justin told *16* magazine, he had his first date and first kiss!)

One of the first friends Justin made was an *MMC* cast mate named JC Chasez. "JC was on the show for four years," Justin explained in *Superteen* magazine, "and I joined two years after that. So, actually, together, we did the show for two years, over on Sound Stage One [at MGM Studios]."

JC took an immediate liking to Justin. "He's very, very athletic and he's just always dying to do things and have a good time," JC told *TV Hits* magazine. "I also love his sincerity—he's a really nice, genuine kind of person." The friendship between JC and Justin led to the two boys sharing their dreams to make it big as musicians. Little did thirteen-year-old Justin and seventeen-year-old JC realize how much bigger and better things would get from there!

Handling Success

Four years later, Justin and JC, joined by Chris Kirkpatrick, Joey Fatone, and Lance Bass, were part of 'N Sync, suddenly one of the most famous groups in the world. The best part of being in 'N Sync, as Justin explained to *TV Hits* magazine, is "being able to make music, meet people and travel." As Justin has pointed out, however, traveling can also have its bad points. "We all get homesick, but we don't really talk about it. Anyway, the five of us are like a family and we all look out for each other."

Though the group's fame has grown to greater heights than Justin ever imagined, he takes it all in stride. "It's growing rapidly and we're very pleased with the progress we've made," he told *16* magazine. "We're nothing but happy and we love our fans." Justin truly adores his fans, as he explained in *Bop* magazine. "To know that you've touched them enough that they listen to your songs so often that they know them by heart—that's special."

Indeed, this is all a dream come true for Justin. As a kid, he idolized Stevie Wonder and, later, as part of an up-and-coming group, he looked up to Boyz II Men. But, as 'N Sync appears to be on their way to achieving the same level of success as Justin's idols, he told *16* magazine that "I don't think that 'N Sync wants to emulate anybody. We want to be pioneers in the music industry. We want to make our own name."

Justin is strikingly mature for his age and has handled fame as well as any teenager could. When one European reporter asked the band members about future solo projects and production efforts after 'N Sync, Justin jumped in, "I don't think that's in any of our heads at this particular moment in time. We're just focusing on 'N Sync at this time. We just want this to be the best that it can possibly be and that's why we're devoting all of our time and attention to this."

Justin doesn't look at himself or his band mates as stars. He sees his band mates as good friends and talented, hardworking musicians. When Justin looks in the mirror he sees an ordinary guy who's been blessed. And, believe it or not, despite the group's success, when Justin looks at 'N Sync, he always sees room for improvement. "When we see ourselves on TV, we start critiquing from the minute we see it, and we want to keep taking steps forward," he told *Teen Beat.*

He may be getting accustomed to his own fame, but Justin still gets starstruck from time to time, like when he found out his group was going to be touring with Janet Jackson. As he recalled to reporters at the Virgin Mega Store opening in New York, "Johnny Wright ['N Sync's manager] just came in and said, 'C'mon man, you're gonna open for Janet Jackson,' and I went, 'Oh, my God!'" Justin, never one to hold back his feelings, added, "See, you don't understand how much I'm in love with Janet Jackson. Probably about two or three years ago I had her poster on my wall, so I'm pretty infatuated." (It makes you wonder if he realizes yet that thousands of people feel that way about *him.*)

Real-Life Justin

Justin still lives with his mom, Lynn, but the two also share their Orlando home (near the band's rehearsal studio) with 'N Sync band mates JC and Chris. Although the guys remain close friends even when they are not working, sometimes Justin gets left behind. Not that he cramps the other guys' styles or anything, it's just that, at seventeen, Justin isn't old enough to get into some of the dance clubs where the older Chris, Joey, JC, and Lance like to go. "I'm a real party animal, when the others let me go to parties," he admitted to *Tiger Beat* magazine. Don't feel too bad, though. Justin's just old enough to drive and recently bought his dream car, a candy apple red Mercedes M class that's "chromed out."

In a *TV Hits* magazine feature, Justin was asked to describe himself in one sentence. "I'm an athletic, nice sorta guy," he said. In person, Justin's one of the most likable people you'll ever meet. He's confident, yet humble. Justin is serious about his music career, but, as his winning smile and infectious laugh will tell you, he never takes himself too seriously. He's just an upbeat guy who really seems to love what he does and who he does it with.

What does the seventeen-year-old pop star

do in his spare time? "I love basketball and whenever I have the chance, I play like crazy," Justin told *Smash Hits* magazine. In case you were wondering, that's where his nickname "Bounce" came from. Justin doesn't just *play* basketball, he watches it on TV, reads about it, and even collects memorabilia. "I collect North Carolina Tarheels basketball gear." Why the University of North Carolina? Two reasons. First, the school's colors are white and baby blue, Justin's favorite color. Second, and more importantly, Justin's idol, pro basketball superstar Michael Jordan, went to UNC and led the team to a National Championship as a freshman.

Justin also loves to watch a good game on TV. Since he lives in Orlando, he's become a big fan of the NBA's Orlando Magic and actively roots for the team and its star player, Penny Hardaway. Justin also likes to dabble in other sports and activities, anything to keep him active. "Working out always puts me in a calmer state of mind," he told *Superteen* magazine.

"I'm also a bit of a shopaholic," Justin confessed to *TV Hits.* He buys mostly CDs and clothes and also collects candles, but is quick to remind everyone within earshot that "my voice is my most prized possession." Like any kid his age, Justin also listens to his CDs, goes to the movies, and watches TV in his spare time.

In case you're wondering, Justin doesn't love everything. He has his share of pet peeves too. For one thing, Justin has made it pretty well known that he is terrified of snakes. In fact, during one interview, his band mates kidded him that there would be a snake on the tour bus and Justin said, "No reptiles! None whatsoever. I will not ride the tour bus!" He also told *16* magazine that if there's one thing that really makes him angry it's "fake people."

One really interesting thing about Justin is that he talks in his sleep. As he told it to *Big Bopper* magazine, "I talk in my sleep a lot. My mom used to laugh at me because if she wanted to find out something about me, she'd come in while I was sleeping and start talking to me." If you ever see Justin sleeping on a plane, just pull up a seat to find out all the secrets that he keeps!

A Student of the Game

Throughout his schooling, Justin was a conscientious student who always got straight A's. He has always been particularly good at math and science and plans to go to college, when his schedule allows for it. As it is, Justin had to earn his high school diploma by completing his senior year through an independent study program.

Justin, who still maintains an interest in acting as well as singing, has felt strongly about college education since his days on *The Mickey Mouse Club.* Back then, he said that a performing arts degree would help him further his career as a singer, comedian, or actor. In the long run, whichever path Justin chooses, success is bound to follow him.

Just the Facts

Full name: Justin Randall Timberlake
Nicknames: Curly; Bounce
Birth date: January 31, 1981

Zodiac sign: Aquarius
Birthplace: Memphis, Tennessee
Height: 6 feet
Weight: 160 pounds
Eye color: Blue
Hair color: Sandy blond
Current residence: Orlando, Florida
Parents: Lynn and stepdad Paul
Siblings: Two younger half brothers, Jonathan and baby Steven
Pets: Dog, Ozzie

Faves:

Singers/Groups: Stevie Wonder; Brian McKnight; Boyz II Men; Take 6
TV shows: *Dawson's Creek; Seinfeld*
Movie: *Ferris Bueller's Day Off*
Actor: Brad Pitt
Actress: Meg Ryan
Book: *Clue*
Food: Pasta
Drink: Milk
Color: Baby blue

Sport: Basketball
Holiday: Christmas
Hobbies: Shopping; going to the movies; working out
Collects: Sneakers
Worst habit: Talks in his sleep
Biggest fear: Snakes
Interesting tidbit: His favorite word is "crunk"—it means crazy

6

jc

Although twenty-two-year-old Washington, D.C., native JC Chasez is often referred to as the lead singer of 'N Sync, he's quick to remind everyone that a team effort is the secret to his group's success. "Everybody's got their own role and is a leader in some respect," he told *TV Hits* magazine. JC's modesty is just part of what makes him so likable. And his steel blue eyes and liquid voice make him absolutely lovable.

JC brings a tireless voice and an all-out, acrobatic energy onstage for every performance, and 'N Sync fans love him for it. Backstage, JC enriches the band with his unstoppable motivation and passion for making music. The motivation comes from his parents and the passion comes from *The Mickey Mouse Club*. Where JC is concerned, it all goes back to his childhood.

D.C. Welcomes JC

Joshua Scott Chasez was born August 8, 1976, in Washington, D.C. Though his parents, Roy and Karen, call him Josh, friends have always called him JC. After moving to nearby Bowie, Maryland, with his family, JC was joined by a younger sister, Heather, and then a brother, Tyler. JC and his siblings enjoyed a suburban childhood complete with elementary school, church, neighborhood friends, and a close-knit family.

JC is proud of his upbringing and isn't at all modest when it comes to bragging about what a good job his parents did raising him and his younger siblings. While a cast member of *The Mickey Mouse Club*, JC told The Disney Channel, "I respect my dad because he respects other people. He takes the time to listen to my point of view." This has stayed with JC, because to this day, his mantra is "Treat people the way you want to be treated."

As fortunate as JC feels about his group's success, he feels even more so about having grown up a part of such a cohesive and stable family. To remind himself of how lucky he is, while with *MMC*, JC devoted much of his free time to volunteer work. Serving meals to the homeless made JC realize, "If you think you have problems, try living on the streets with your family," as he told The Disney Channel.

JC & The Sunshine Band

As a young boy, JC had boundless energy. Playing sports was a good outlet for JC early on, but later, he would find dancing to be an even better one. He'd loved listening to music since he was a toddler, but as he got older he realized that dancing was not only a great way to enjoy music, but it was also something for him to throw all of that extra energy into.

"When music was introduced to me for the first time, I fell in love immediately," JC recalled in the liner notes of 'N Sync's debut album. "Thanks to a great many people, my love for it grows stronger every day." JC knew his calling and, at the age of 13, shortly after he and his family moved to Florida, he joined the cast of

The Mickey Mouse Club. Around the same time, he began street dancing with a teen group in national competitions.

JC enjoyed the acting and comedy of *MMC* and he learned to feel more and more comfortable with television exposure and live performances. But more than anything, JC loved to dance. He practiced night and day, both with dance groups and on his own. Gymnastics classes improved his flexibility and helped him expand his dancing repertoire to include acrobatic stunts like tumbles and flips, which he now incorporates into his 'N Sync performances.

JC also found another way to embrace his love for music: singing. "I didn't start singing until I got to Orlando with *The Mickey Mouse Club,*" he told *Superteen* magazine. "I didn't know that much about music. I just knew that I liked to dance and I started singing cover tunes." After lots of practice and brushing up with a vocal coach, JC began singing during stage performances at Disney World. By his third year with *The Mickey Mouse Club*, JC gained enough confidence to begin singing solo.

Being a Mouseketeer was just the springboard that JC needed. "It was one of the best things I could have done," JC said in *Teen Beat* magazine. "I got to get my fingers into everything—I wasn't restricted to one thing at all. I got to do comedy, which was fun, and I got to do all kinds of music. If I could do it again, I would."

During his third season, JC ran into the newest member of *MMC*, Justin Timberlake. Through working together on the show and with the same vocal coach, the two became great friends. After their last season (JC's fourth and Justin's second) on *MMC* ended, Justin and JC found themselves at the same Nashville studio, working on separate solo projects. After some discussions, and some impromptu harmonies, a seed was planted. When a few other seeds by the names of Chris, Joey, and Lance were added, the quintet blossomed into quite an act.

Success Hasn't Spoiled Him Yet

From 'N Sync's early struggles to their current stardom, JC's favorite thing about the group remains the same. As he told *Bop* magazine, "The best thing about being in the band is the friendship—having people around you so you're never lonely."

Fame and fortune are secondary to JC. To him it always comes back to the music. "The beauty of music is that everyone hears it their own way," JC added in the album insert, "and every song you hear leaves an impression on you that alters the way you hear everything from that point on." JC especially appreciates pop music because of its wide appeal. "It used to be thought of as bubble gum, but it's not anymore," he explained to *Tiger Beat* magazine. "The best thing about pop is that it has a little bit of everything in it. Pop can really go in any direction."

When it comes to making a record, it's all about the music, and when it comes to performing, to JC, it's all about the fans. To date, there hasn't been a single 'N Sync television appearance or magazine or radio interview where JC didn't show his appreciation for the group's fans. In fact, as a constant reminder of how important 'N Sync's fans are to the group's success, JC treasures many of the gifts he receives from fans. "I usually keep a stuffed animal from a show to sleep on while we're traveling," he admitted to *TV Hits* magazine.

The truest indicator of how well JC handles fame is the way he constantly diverts attention from himself. Anytime a music critic or entertainment reporter asks JC a question about something he did, he always responds with a "we" or an "us" answer. If JC has a fault, it's that he doesn't know how to take a compliment. Say one nice thing about him and he'll start talking about how talented and wonderful his band mates are.

By the way, JC may be humble, but he is human. He rewarded himself by buying a new Jeep with one of his first big paychecks.

What's JC Like, Anyway?

Above all else, JC is focused. "He's hard-working and dedicated and a very serious sort of person," Chris spilled to *TV Hits* magazine. "I don't mean he's not any fun, but he knows when it's time to play and when it's time to work. He's really dedicated to his career and that's really admirable."

JC often takes on the role of keeping the other 'N Syncers in line. But, like his band mates, JC also makes an effort to not take himself too seriously. "I'm not bossy, I'm just in order" is how JC jokingly described himself to *Live & Kicking* magazine.

It's a good thing JC has a sense of humor, otherwise he'd never be able to withstand the constant ribbing from his band mates about everything from his basketball skills to how he goes about meeting girls. "JC's just cheesy," Chris spilled to *TV Hits* magazine. "He's got all these really bad pickup lines and, I promise that the other day, he actually said to this girl, 'So, do you come here often?' "

JC's fellow 'N Syncers also never let him rest about his sleep habits. "You see, JC matured too quickly," Joey kidded with a British reporter. "He peaked at the age of fifteen and he's going downhill slowly. All he wants to do now is sleep!"

"I'm a pretty heavy sleeper," JC admitted to *Big Bopper* magazine. "I fell asleep on the plane and we landed and everything and I didn't know it. Lance had to smack me on the back of the head and go, 'Dude, the plane is empty. You're the last one.' I said, 'Oh, my goodness.'"

JC has a sense of humor about it too, having admitted that his Spice name would be "Sleepy Spice." With the schedule he must maintain, who could blame him? "You go through the day sleeping 15 minutes here, 20 minutes there," he explained in *BB* magazine. "If I sit down for long, my body goes, 'Okay, you're not tired, but you know what? You need to rest just in case.'"

Aside from enjoying a good catnap, JC loves to listen to music and he has quite a variety of CDs in his collection—Sting, Seal, Robyn, Stevie Wonder, Billie Holiday, Brian McKnight, and Boyz II Men, to name but a few. "Sting and Seal are both tremendous song writers," he told *Smash Hits* magazine. JC also lifts weights and watches a bit of TV, especially when his favorite football team, the Washington Redskins, are on. "I love the movies and anything that keeps me fit, especially in-line skating," JC told *Teen Machine* magazine.

Is there anything that gets under JC's skin? You bet. He admits to being terrified of needles (no pun intended) and he also says that if there's one thing he can't stand it's a liar. But then, what would you expect from a good, honest person?

Just the Facts

Full name: Joshua Scott Chasez
Nickname: JC
Birth date: August 8, 1976
Zodiac sign: Leo
Birthplace: Washington, D.C.
Height: 5 feet 10 inches
Weight: 150 pounds
Eye color: Blue
Hair color: Brown
Current residence: Orlando, Florida
Parents: Karen and Roy
Siblings: One younger brother, Tyler (sixteen), and one younger sister, Heather (twenty)
Pets: Cat, Grendal

Faves:

Singers/Groups: Brian McKnight, Robyn, Boyz II Men, Sting, Seal
TV show: *South Park*
Movies: *The Fifth Element, Star Wars*
Actor: Harrison Ford
Actress: Meg Ryan
Book: *The Hobbit*
Food: Chinese food
Drink: Water, iced tea
Color: Black
Sports: In-line skating; football; weight lifting
Holiday: Christmas

Hobbies: Sleeping; going to the movies; listening to CDs
Collects: Hard Rock Cafe menus from around the world
Worst habit: Bites his nails
Biggest fear: Needles
Interesting tidbit: Was on *MMC* with *Felicity*'s Keri Russell

7
chris

If 'N Sync has a class clown it's definitely Chris Kirkpatrick. The twenty-seven-year-old Pennsylvania native may be the oldest member of the group, but he is by no means the most reserved. Chris is all business when it's time to perform, rehearse, or record, but when the work is done, he puts his party hat on. Just as no deck of cards is complete without a joker, no band is complete without a comic relief, and Chris takes on this ridiculously valuable role in 'N Sync.

After a long day on the road, when the guys are tired, homesick, and even cranky, it definitely helps to have a court jester around to lighten things up a bit. "It's your best quality," Lance told him during an interview. "When you're crazy, you're funny and that makes people laugh and it's really cool."

Onstage and in 'N Sync's videos, Chris is a chameleon. From one song to the next you never know what to expect. Chris varies hair styles and color, facial hair and clothing. He even knows how to accessorize, with the wide array of jewelry, hats, and bandannas he's known to sport. It goes without saying, of course, but Chris can sing and dance with the best of 'em too. And there's nothing in the world he'd rather do.

From One Family to Another

When Christopher Alan Kirkpatrick was born on October 17, 1971, he was a far cry from the wild-haired, rambunctious guy he is now. The precious baby boy was the pride and joy of his mom, Bev, who first coddled Chris at home in a suburban Pittsburgh town called Clarion, Pennsylvania. Chris and his family eventually moved to Dalton, Ohio, where he attended public school.

Chris's upbringing was not as simple as it was for his band mates. He was later joined by four younger half sisters and his father passed away when he was young. Chris calls this his "worst memory." In addition to the five women in his life, Chris also considers his band mates family. In fact, now, Chris shares a home with JC, Justin, and Justin's mom in Orlando.

Music was an important part of growing up for Chris. "I know that when I was born I pretty much was singing," he recalled in *Teen Beat* magazine. "My mom said I could sing before I could talk, so I don't know if that means I couldn't talk, but I just know that I've always loved music and loved listening to music and performing."

Chris continued singing after he graduated high school, joining his college choir group and singing in area coffee shops to earn extra money. "I've been to college—been there done that," he told *Tiger Beat* magazine. "I actually graduated from Valencia College with my associate of arts degree, and then I transferred to Rollins College [in Boca Raton, Florida]."

While a student at Rollins, Chris got a job at Universal Studios. "I used to sing with a '50s doo-wop group called the Hollywood High

Tones," he recalled in *Superteen* magazine. "We used to sing outside the '50s diner at Universal. That was me—it was three guys and one girl and we'd sing '50s a cappella music. My name was Spike, but my hair was a little different then." While working the gig, Chris befriended a performer named Joey Fatone, who also worked at Universal. Joey knew a guy named JC at Disney and one thing led to another, and the next thing Chris knew, he was in a real band.

"Then they kicked me out of class to do the group," he joked with *16* magazine. "No, they didn't really kick me out. I had to drop out of Rollins because of the group. I didn't have time to do college and the group."

Lovin' Every Minute of It

To Chris, the best thing about being a part of 'N Sync is "seeing my musical ideas come to life and meeting new people in new places." In fact, Chris enjoys all the excitement so much that "sometimes I get more homesick when I'm at home—I miss all the touring," he told *Smash Hits* magazine.

He also loves and admires the other members of 'N Sync. Although Chris says Michael Jackson was his boyhood idol, he now gets his musical inspiration from his band mates. "I know how hard they work and their reasons for doing it. I just think they're incredible." During an America Online interview, Chris was asked about the secret to his success. His answer? "Justin, JC, Lance, Joey."

Chris also adores the group's growing number of fans and took the opportunity to remind the fans of how important they are in the European debut CD's liner notes. "Last but not least, I would like to thank the sixth member of 'N Sync—the fans. Without you, we could not have made this dream a reality."

It didn't take Chris long to realize that being in a touring band wasn't all fame and fanfare. "We've got crazy hours," Chris said in *Bop* magazine, "but I've learned to sleep on airplanes a lot and in vans."

Crazy Like a Fox

"Chris is probably the funniest," JC told *Smash Hits* magazine. "I think everybody has their moments, but Chris just seems to have more of them." Chris corrected him, "I think we're all equally funny—It's just I come out of the box the fastest." Aside from making his band mates laugh, Chris loves to crack *himself* up. He thinks one of the funniest things in the world is telling people jokes that don't make any sense, laughing at them, and then waiting to see if they laugh too.

If you think he's weird, you're not the only one. "Chris is the crazy one," JC told *Smash Hits* magazine. "Yeah, he's a coupla sandwiches short of a picnic!" Lance added.

Chris makes no attempt to mask his silly side and freely admits to being a bit gonzo. "I'm crazy and outgoing," Chris told *Live & Kicking* magazine. "I'm the most hyper member of the group. I need lots of calming down." What does this bizarre behavior stem from? "I have a really short attention span, so things tend to bore me easily, which I hate," Chris explained in *Teen Machine* magazine.

Warm It Up, Chris!

Aside from being wild and crazy, Chris has interests, likes and dislikes, just like us normal folks. "I like beaches and I live near one," Chris calmly explained in an America Online interview, before adding that he once went surfing during a hurricane! Chris also likes to in-line skate and play basketball. When indoors, he plays Sony PlayStation games, cracks up over episodes of *South Park*, and "spins records." "I love writing and listening to music so I've invested in a laptop to make life easier," he told *TV Hits* magazine.

Chris also devotes his energies to maintaining his rather unique personal style. "I just like what's comfortable, skater stuff," was how he described his wardrobe in *All-Stars* magazine. Chris's hair, however, has definitely been one point of contention. It has gone from pageboy to very long bangs to dreadlocks in just a year. He also has quite a collection of bandannas, sunglasses, jewelry, and sports jerseys. Chris digs clothing by Calvin Klein, partly because he likes the styles, but also because he and the famous designer share the same initials. One little-known fact: Chris sometimes wears glasses.

Just the Facts

Full name: Christopher Alan Kirkpatrick
Nicknames: Chris; Lucky
Birth date: October 17, 1971
Zodiac sign: Libra
Birthplace: Clarion, Pennsylvania
Height: 5 feet 9 inches
Weight: 155 pounds
Eye color: Brown
Hair color: Brown
Current residence: Orlando, Florida
Parents: Mom, Bev
Siblings: Four younger half sisters: Molly, Kate, Emily, and Taylor
Pets: None

Faves:

Singers/Groups: Brian McKnight; The Beatles
TV show: *South Park*
Movie: *Happy Gilmore*
Actor: George Clooney
Actress: Audrey Hepburn
Book: *Dragon Lance*
Food: Tacos; chocolate ice cream
Drink: Orange juice; milk
Color: Silver
Sports: Football; basketball; hockey
Holiday: Halloween

Hobbies: Going to the beach; in-line skating; Sony PlayStation
Collects: Records
Worst habit: Staying up too late
Biggest fear: Heights
Interesting tidbit: He went to high school with Howie Dorough of the Backstreet Boys

8

joey

If 'N Sync ever wins a Grammy Award, you can bet Joey will be the one to take so long thanking every person he's ever met that his band mates will have to drag him offstage. This is not just because he is the most talkative member of the group, but also because he is probably the most gracious. In fact, "thank you" is probably the phrase Joey utters the most. In 'N Sync's European debut CD's liner notes, Joey thanks just about everybody he can think of, including family, friends, band mates, record industry people, the fans and media, and then adds, "To all of the above and the many people I did not mention, I love you and all the thanks in the world!"

Joey brings so much to 'N Sync that it's hard to imagine the quintet without him. His dancing and singing talents, optimism, sense of humor, and boundless ambition are all invaluable to the group. Joey grew up with music in his veins but still had to come a long way, from New York to Florida and from high school to superstardom, in a very short period of time. Here's how it all began.

Brooklyn Boy Makes Good

Born and raised in Brooklyn, New York, Joseph Anthony Fatone, Jr., was the product of a typical Catholic, Italian-American upbringing, replete with a large but close-knit extended family and an emphasis on religion, morals, and good home cooking. When Joey, Sr., and Phyllis Fatone gave birth to Joey, Jr., on January 28, 1977, he was the third child in the family, joining older siblings Janine, now twenty-seven, and Steven, now twenty-five.

Throughout his childhood, Joey was surrounded by tons of people who cared about him. Perhaps that helps explain why he's such a nice guy. Joey played with neighborhood kids after school, enjoyed dinners with his family, and went to church on Sunday. Holidays were a big deal in the Fatone family, especially Christmas, when his enormous extended family would get together. Justin has said that Joey has so many aunts, uncles, and cousins that his phone never stops ringing. "He's Italian and he has *family,*" Justin explained during an interview with *16* magazine, before doing his best imitation of Joey's New York accent.

Music always played a part in Joey's life. "My parents listened to a lot of older '50s music and that's what first influenced me," Joey recalled in *All-Stars* magazine. "My sister and I were always singing around the house and being loud." Joey's initial inspiration came from his father. "He used to sing in a group called the Orions. They weren't famous, but they were great. They had records and stuff and every time they played, I would be singing and stuff like that behind my dad."

Before Joey could begin high school, his family decided to move to Florida. "Growing up, every time there was a vacation, we'd come down to Florida," Joey explained in *Teen Beat*

(Anthony Cutajar/London Features)

(Rudolphe Baras/London Features)

Joey

justin

(Rudolphe Baras/London Features)

(Todd Kaplan/Star File)

Tearin' Up *Your* Heart

(Paul Fenton/Shooting Star)

(Paul Fenton/Shooting Star)

JC

lance

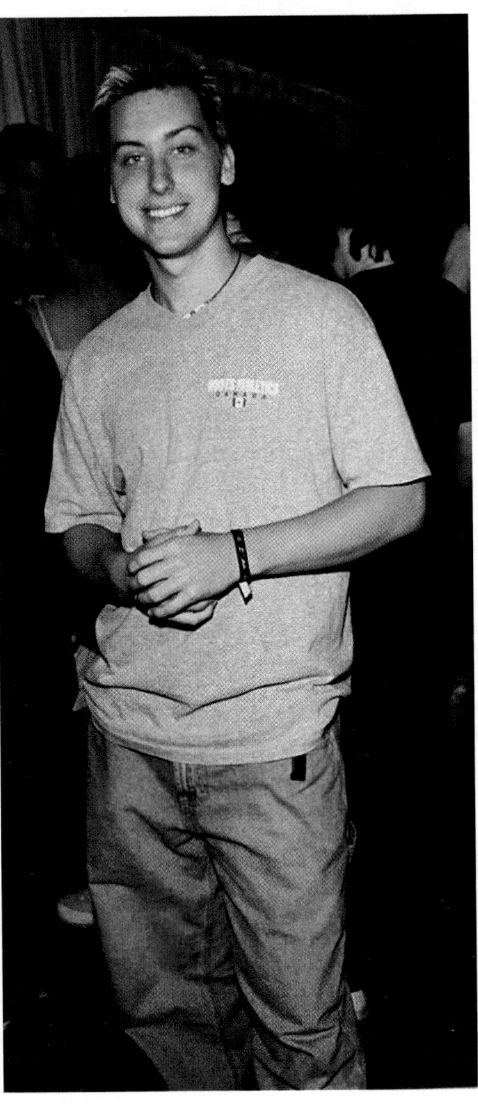

(Paul Fenton/Shooting Star)

(Rodolphe Baras/London Features)

CHRIS

(Todd Kaplan/Star File)

(Anthony Cutajar/London Features

magazine. "When a certain neighborhood and the area was getting a little bit bad my family wanted to move to Florida. It's sunny all the time and nice. The houses were a little bit cheaper and there was actually more space. Orlando's always developing. We moved about six or seven years ago."

Joey attended high school in the Orlando area, where he made new friends and developed an interest in dancing. "In high school when I tried to do musicals, that's when I pretty much got involved with dancing," Joey recalled in *Superteen* magazine. "I took a little bit of jazz, a little ballet, I *tried* to do tap but . . ."

High school offered quite a bit to Joey. In fact, while he was there, not only did he learn how to dance, but he took up acting. According to his record company bio, Joey appeared in small roles in the movies *Once Upon a Time in America* and *Matinee* as well as on the TV series *SeaQuest.* Toward the end of high school Joey joined an a cappella singing group and began honing his singing voice, and all of a sudden it was time to grow up.

"My best moment was graduating high school," Joey fondly recalled in *Tiger Beat* magazine. "It was great. It was sad, but it was happy because everybody that I grew up with over the four years was going off to college and everything to start a career, and this is what we started and I've been happy ever since."

Uprooted, Upbeat, Unstoppable

"My parents have been very supportive of me," Joey told *Teen Beat* magazine. "They think it's wonderful. They've backed us up from the very beginning and I love them for it and thank them." Upon graduation, Joey took a job at a nearby theme park and met some important people. "I've known JC ever since I moved here. I used to go to high school with some of the people who were on *The Mickey Mouse Club* and he was on it too. Then I met Chris from working at Universal Studios."

"At Universal, I did a show called *The Beetlejuice Graveyard Review* and I played characters like the Wolfman and Dracula," Joey explained in a *16* magazine interview, but was sure not to belittle the experience. "We did entertainment. As far as that goes, entertainment is entertainment. It's always performing on stage or performing in front of an audience, and that's what we're doing and that's what we love doing. That was our jobs then, and it's our jobs now."

"I feel most comfortable on stage or in front of the camera," Joey said in *16* magazine. "No matter what I do, I go at it full-tilt and can't be stopped." This attitude went a long way toward Joey's current gig as a member of 'N Sync. Only now, performing in front of thousands at sold-out arenas is a bit different from putting on a show for hundreds at a theme park. "A lot more people know you," he explained in *Teen Machine* magazine. "Instead of saying you were this on this stage, now you are Joey. It's you up there."

A number of magazines have asked each of the 'N Sync guys what they think is the best thing about being in the band. Typically, Joey has two answers. He told one American magazine, "Definitely the travel. I love visiting different places." His answer for one British magazine was that his mission was to "Go up onstage and turn around the world!"

Now, Joey's career is moving at the speed of light and he and his band mates are constantly a center of attention. "It's all happening so quickly. It still hasn't hit us yet," he remarked in *All-Stars* magazine. After all, one minute he's Joey from Brooklyn, the next he's Joey from 'N Sync. "It is pretty flattering, actually, when people say, 'Oh, you're that person in 'N Sync. I know who you are,'" he told *Bop* magazine.

But Joey won't let it go to his head. "We're still normal guys. It's always fun being recognized and everything which is wonderful, but we're just normal guys. We keep each other in check, and make sure our feet are always on the ground. What you see is what you get."

Joey takes the bad with the good and has learned to deal with things like getting homesick. "When you're on the road you're so busy you don't get time to think about it," he told *16* magazine. "You just get on with it."

Just Joey

"Joey definitely talks the most," Chris told *TV Hits* magazine. "Once he starts, he just goes rambling on and he doesn't stop for breath. It all ends up being one huge, long sentence, like this, and you find yourself trying to breathe for him!" He may be a bit of a chatterbox, but Joey has some righteous things to say.

"Joey's a very optimistic person," Justin explained. "Whenever things aren't going too good, he'll really try his hardest to make them better."

"I cheer the guys up when they get down," Joey told one European magazine. He's really happy with his life and career and it shows. He just hopes that some of his optimism will rub off on others. "I'm outgoing and try to make people laugh," Joey told *Live & Kicking* magazine.

So, what kinds of things does Joey like? "I love Superman memorabilia and collect the T-shirts, jewelry—anything and everything," he told *Superteen* magazine. "I also love dancing and going to clubs. I like sports, but aside from skating I'm useless at sports." Joey also loves going to the movies and dancing at clubs. "Sometimes me and Chris want to go out and party all night," Joey confessed in *TV Hits* magazine.

Joey also has a bit of a hankering for funky clothes. "He does have a style, but it's out there," Chris explained in *Superstars* magazine. "He's got crazy stuff! He's got one coat that looks like he killed Chewbacca and one red suit that makes him look like Elmo. And his jeans are humongous!"

"I've got one pair with fiber optics down the side and they light up," Joey added. "And I like to wear tight Superman shirts."

Joey also digs Italian food, R&B music, watching *South Park*, and almost anything that's purple. There's only one thing for sure he doesn't like. As he's told more than one reporter, "The thing that I hate most of all is fake people."

Just the Facts

Full name: Joseph Anthony Fatone, Jr.
Nicknames: Joey; Phat 1; Superman

Birth date: January 28, 1977
Zodiac sign: Aquarius
Birthplace: Brooklyn, New York
Height: 6 feet
Weight: 175 pounds
Eye color: Brown
Hair color: Brown
Current residence: Orlando, Florida
Parents: Phyllis and Joe
Siblings: One older brother, Steven, and one older sister, Janine
Pets: None

Faves:

Singer/Group: Boyz II Men
TV show: *South Park*
Movie: *Willy Wonka and the Chocolate Factory*
Actor: Robert De Niro
Actress: Sandra Bullock
Book: Shakespeare's play *Macbeth*
Food: Italian
Drink: Soft drinks

Color: Purple
Sports: "I'm useless at sports"
Holiday: Christmas
Hobbies: Going to the movies, dancing at clubs
Collects: Superman memorabilia
Worst habit: Talking too much
Biggest fear: "I don't have one"
Interesting tidbit: Likes '50s doo-wop music

9

lance

Lovable Lance Bass was the fifth and final member to join 'N Sync, but by no means does this make him the least important. In fact, his band mates, who admit they didn't sound quite right without him, consider Lance's deep bass to have been the missing piece to the 'N Sync puzzle. Lance also brings a sense of responsibility far beyond his years to the group. "Lance has always got the schedule down pat," JC told *TV Hits* magazine. "He's always on top of things."

"The guys call me 'Scoop' cuz whenever they ask me about our itinerary, I always know," Lance boasted to *Live & Kicking* magazine.

Lance, or "Lansten," as his band mates prefer to call him, is definitely the shiest member of the group, but he's always up for a good time. Nowhere does he enjoy himself more than up onstage where his voice, grooves, and movie-star good looks make him a key ingredient in the 'N Sync mix.

From Home Cookin' to Arena Bookin'

Lance came a very long way from where he was just a few years ago, and not just in the geographical sense. Where Justin, JC, Chris, and Joey were concerned, they were on course to make it in the music business. For Lance, the opportunity to be a professional musician, let alone a pop star, came completely by surprise and swept him off his feet.

James Lance Bass was born on May 4, 1979, in Clinton, Mississippi. Parents Diane and Jim brought their bundle of joy back to their semi-rural home, where they were already raising three-year-old daughter Stacy. As a sweet, fair-haired boy, Lance—as he was called—played sports, went to school, and attended church. "I grew up singing in church and I always loved singing," Lance recalled in *Teen Machine* magazine. The southern boy grew up on country-

and-western music, though his musical taste has since expanded.

While a boy, Lance dreamed of being an astronaut. As he got older, Lance began showing a passionate determination in his studies, getting straight A's all the way through high school. He continued singing, began dating, and got more serious about his childhood dream. "I wanted to go into space administration," he told *Teen Beat* magazine. "Probably not an astronaut but something in that field."

Also while in high school, Lance began working on his singing with a vocal coach. As his singing improved, Lance started having thoughts about another career, as an entertainer. Though his parents supported his interests, they had their doubts. Lance continued to study hard and get the grades and was accepted to the University of Nebraska. He was all set to go to college and study science, make new friends, and live in a dorm room. Then one day, during his senior year, a phone call came that would change his life.

"I always wanted to sing professionally, but I

didn't think that I would have the chance until they called me up. Right when they called me up was when I was like, 'Okay!'" The person on the other end of that fateful phone call was Lance's vocal coach, who also happened to be coaching Justin Timberlake and knew that there was an immediate need for a bass vocalist down in Florida. "When they called me to join the group, I immediately moved down to Orlando," Lance told *Teen Beat* magazine.

What about his dream to be an astronaut and fly the space shuttle? "Yeah, I was seriously thinking about it," he recalled in *All-Stars* magazine. "That's what I was doing up until I left for Orlando and joined the group." Surely Lance's parents must have had a say in this, right? "Once they saw that it was the real thing, they weren't going to stop me," Lance proudly admitted. "I finished high school through independent study."

Lance knows full well that without the unconditional support of his family, he never could have followed his dream. In the liner notes of the European release of 'N Sync's debut CD, Lance took the time to show his sincere gratitude. "I want to say thank you to my mom, dad and my sister, Stacy, for their support, love and many sacrifices they had to make throughout the early stages of 'N Sync."

Despite his life being turned upside down by joining 'N Sync, and despite the group's grueling schedule, Lance enrolled as a freshman at the University of Nebraska anyway. So far, he's managed to take only a few classes, but he does plan to get a degree. It may take more than four years, though, since fame came calling. "I'm in my freshman year of college and it's really hard," Lance said in *Teen Beat* magazine. "I'm taking it one step at a time and I'm trying to get settled with that."

With so many talents, an exciting future in entertainment, and a great support group of friends and family behind him, there isn't much Lance can't do. Plus, as Joey pointed out in *All-Stars* magazine, "He's really interested in business and marketing and is always on top of things. He could be a business manager some day."

Or an astronaut.

Hitting the Big Time

Lance's best advice to other aspiring musicians is to "never give up, practice and get a good manager," as he said in an America Online interview. It certainly proved to be the right formula for him. His ideals are the same, but since his world was rocked by the opportunity of a lifetime, Lance has different goals. Now, as part of a famous pop group, Lance has two objectives—to win a Grammy Award and to have the chance to meet his favorite country singer, Garth Brooks.

To Lance, the best thing about being a part of 'N Sync is "being on stage, performing and seeing all of the people and watching them enjoying and reacting to our music," he told *TV Hits Australia* magazine. And, boy, does Lance love 'N Sync fans! Perhaps the reason why he can relate to his fans so well is because Lance fondly remembers when he himself was a starstruck kid who treasured autographs and memorabilia. "I've got the weirdest things in the world, like little autographs on a napkin that I framed . . . because it was such a big deal to me," he reminisced in *Bop* magazine.

Lance has gotten a taste of the negative side of celebrity as well. Through firsthand experience he can tell you living the glamorous life means hard work, little sleep, and lots of attention. Throughout it all, as a celebrity you have to always be careful not to put your foot in your mouth. "We get to do different interviews," Lance explained in *Superteen* magazine. "We're like, 'Why did we say that?' We look at it and we kind of critique ourselves for the next time. It's a learning experience for us."

Above all else though, Lance remains positive. When asked by *Superstars* magazine what he wanted for his birthday, Lance replied, "A number one album." (Well, Lance, your timing's a bit off, but it could be a merry Christmas.)

Pleased to Meet You, Lance

When a reporter for *TV Hits* magazine asked 'N Sync who the shiest member of the group was, the likely candidate ironically stepped forward and answered, "Me, probably." Lance went on to explain his timid ways. "I'm all right once I know people, but at first I find it really hard."

Lance may be outwardly shy, but certainly not for any lack of confidence. Just ask Joey, who told one British reporter, "Lance uses us like wild dogs—he holds us by the leash and waits for us to go sniff people out and then he goes and meets them himself." Accordingly, this isn't far from how Lance goes about flirting with girls. "He's pretty good at it and he's sneaky with it too," Chris spilled. "You don't really know he's doing it till bam, it's too late."

Lance fits right in down in sunny, easygoing Florida, where he lives in Orlando with his parents, "just a mile away from the other guys." He often describes himself as "laid-back and friendly." Justin seconds that notion. "Lance is really laid back," he offered at a teen press conference. "JC's always moving around, but Lance doesn't really do that. He just chills."

As JC, Chris, Joey, and Justin will certainly

attest, Lance is a great friend. "He's a really good person to talk to," Joey told *TV Hits* magazine. The four band mates are careful not to pay Lance too many compliments, though; it makes him blush.

As good-looking and talented as Lance is, he's so modest it's astounding. "I can't bear looking in the mirror," he told *Live & Kicking* magazine. "I guess that's why my hair looks like this!" (If only we all looked so terrible when we rolled out of bed!) Lance is, admittedly, not a morning person. "The worst feeling in the world is waking up in the morning," he said in one early interview. Once he's up and about, picking out clothes isn't much of a chore for Lance. "I go through preppy and sporty stages," he told *Teen Beat* magazine.

What does Lance do in his free time? "I love the beach," Lance told one British magazine. "In fact I'm the biggest beach bum and have the legs to prove it—my hairs are bleached blond!" He's also quite hi-tech, spending time on the Internet and playing video games. Like Justin and JC, Lance is also into sports, but he prefers "the more adventurous stuff like rock climbing, skydiving and Jet Skiing."

What brings a frown to Lance's face? He summed up all of his dislikes in one sentence for *TV Hits Australia* magazine: "I'm not into rap, people who pre-judge you or mushrooms."

Just the Facts

Full name: James Lance Bass
Nicknames: Lansten; Scoop
Birth date: May 4, 1979
Zodiac sign: Taurus
Birthplace: Clinton, Mississippi
Height: 5 feet 10 inches
Weight: 155 pounds
Eye color: Green
Hair color: Blond
Current residence: Orlando, Florida
Parents: Diane and Jim
Siblings: One older sister, Stacy
Pets: None

Faves:

Singers/Groups: Garth Brooks; Matchbox 20
TV show: *3rd Rock from the Sun*
Movie: *Titanic*
Actor: Tom Hanks
Actress: Helen Hunt
Book: *The Outsiders*
Food: French toast; Mexican food
Drink: Dr Pepper
Color: Red
Sports: Rock climbing; skydiving
Holiday: Christmas

Hobbies: Going to the beach; Jet Skiing; Sony PlayStation; going on-line
Collects: Tazmanian Devil stuff
Worst habit: Has been known to sleepwalk
Biggest fear: "Things that buzz"
Interesting tidbit: Wishes he was taller

10

shout out to the fans

During the first half of 1998, millions of fans worldwide helped make 'N Sync a chart-topping, platinum-selling band, by buying their debut album, showing up at their appearances in droves, and tuning in to their televised specials. To return the favor, Justin, JC, Lance, Chris, and Joey decided to devote the second half of the year to their fans.

The fans would receive a number of thank-yous from their favorite band, beginning in October with the start of 'N Sync's first major U.S. concert tour. 'N Sync was the opening act for Janet Jackson on the East Coast leg of her tour. All eight concerts—in Baltimore, Chicago, Detroit, Raleigh, Virginia Beach, Atlantic City, Memphis, and New Orleans—sold out.

The fab five followed this up with seventeen headlining concerts from November 19 to

December 13. Up-and-coming young singer Brittany Spears (also a *Mickey Mouse Club* alum) and the hot girl group Wild Orchid were the opening acts. The whirlwind tour took 'N Sync from their native Florida up the East Coast and through the Midwest in just twenty-five days.

'N Sync in Concert

Audiences at 'N Sync concerts are treated to lively, visual, and fun performances by five young guys who really seem to love putting on a show for their fans. "We want the best live show," JC told *Teen Beat* magazine prior to the tour. "We want people to leave there going, 'man, that was so cool!'" Well, the fans who were lucky enough to catch 'N Sync on their 1998 tour certainly got their money's worth as each concert featured light shows, choreographed dance routines, costume changes, cover songs, and even audience participation, as JC would encourage the crowds to sing along with the group!

At this point, the guys don't get too nervous before a big show but still must prepare themselves before taking the stage. "We always pray before a concert and we always give each other hugs," Lance told *Tiger Beat* magazine. "On tours we always play hackey sack before a show. We have to delay the show sometimes, because we're not very good. We'll have to come up with some new rituals."

"The hackey sack thing started off as like a joke," Justin explained. "But, it became this superstitious thing towards the middle of our tour. We're all like, 'We can't go onstage until we make this hackey.'" A hackey is when three different players in the circle touch the sack before it hits the ground. As with performing, the guys have improved their play with experience.

'N Sync 1998 Tour Schedule

Opening for Janet Jackson

October 14 — The Arena
Baltimore, Maryland

October 16	Rosemont Horizon Chicago, Illinois
October 18	Palace Theatre Detroit, Michigan
October 20	Walnut Creek Raleigh, North Carolina
October 21	The Amphitheatre Virginia Beach, Virginia
October 23	Cultural Center Theatre Scranton, Pennsylvania
October 24	Palace Hartford, Connecticut
October 25	Taj Mahal Atlantic City, New Jersey
October 27	The Pyramid Memphis, Tennessee
October 28	Superdome New Orleans, Louisiana

'N Sync Headlining

November 18	Tupperware Center Orlando, Florida
November 19	Sundome Tampa, Florida

November 20	County Fair Broward County, Florida
November 22	Fox Theatre Atlanta, Georgia
November 24	Landmark Theatre Richmond, Virginia
November 25	Music Fair Westbury, New York
December 1	Veterans Memorial Columbus, Ohio
December 2	State Theatre Kalamazoo, Michigan
December 3	Murat Theatre Indianapolis, Indiana
December 4	Lakewood Cleveland, Ohio
December 5	Royal Oak Detroit, Michigan
December 8	Riverside Theatre Milwaukee, Wisconsin
December 9	American St. Louis, Missouri
December 10	Ryman Auditorium Nashville, Tennessee

December 11	Memorial Hall Kansas City, Kansas
December 13	Palace Theatre Louisville, Kentucky

Appearance Is Everything

Before, during, and after the tour, 'N Sync made about a dozen television appearances at the end of 1998. They promoted their album and tour on a number of national talk shows, including *The Tonight Show with Jay Leno* and *The View* in September, and then on *The Ricki Lake Show* in October. At press time they were also scheduled to appear on a float in the annual Macy's Thanksgiving Day Parade, which is televised nationally.

To show they were in the holiday spirit, 'N Sync was part of three different televised Christmas specials in December. Since they would be on tour in December, the specials were taped in October. First up was *The Disney Channel Christmas Special* on December 5. As a follow-up to their wildly successful *'N Sync In*

Concert special, the guys performed along with Monica, Usher, and Shawn Colvin. Next they did the *Kathie Lee Christmas* special, which aired on CBS the week of Christmas. The final show was the *ABC Walt Disney World Christmas Special,* which aired on Christmas day as a special treat for young viewers across America.

A Christmas Present to the Fans

Since Justin, JC, Lance, Chris, and Joey had as much fun on the tour as the crowds did, it was hard for them to call that a gift to their fans. Just before the fab five began their tour, they worked overtime to finish up two projects that would be all but gift-wrapped for their fans in time for Christmas. Both the 'N Sync home video and the *Home for Christmas* holiday album came out on November 10, 1998, and quickly landed in Christmas stockings all over the world.

"Our Christmas CD is coming out in November and it's going to be awesome," JC gushed to reporters late last summer at the

Virgin Mega Store opening. He was particularly excited about one collaboration on the new album. "The K-Ci & JoJo tune is awesome. It's my favorite so far," he added.

Home for Christmas includes 12 tracks: four traditional holiday songs and eight brand-new holiday tunes. 'N Sync put their own spin on classics like "The First Noel," "The Christmas Song," "O Holy Night," and "This Christmas," at the same time they introduced the world to eight new jingles that could make yuletide history. "I Never Knew the Meaning of Christmas," "Love's in Our Hearts on Christmas Day," "Under My Tree," "I Hear Angels," "Will You Be Mine This Christmas?," "It's Christmas," "In Love on Christmas," and "Home for Christmas" all unite romance and holiday cheer in smooth sing-along ballads.

Years from now, when 'N Sync fans are singing these holiday tunes to their children, they'll remember that *Home for Christmas* was just a great band's way of saying thanks.

11

what's 'N Store for 'N Sync?

So, what does a new band who put out a multi-platinum debut album, three hit singles, a sold-out concert tour, and several highly rated TV specials do for an encore in 1999? Stay busy and stay on top. "We're pretty much booked until the spring [of 1999]," Justin told *16* magazine.

The American concert tour was expected to keep 'N Sync busy right up until Christmas. At that point, the fab five all hoped to spend some quiet time on the home front back in Orlando with their families. With the start of the new year and considering the group's worldwide success and their fans' appetite for more, 'N Sync has a number of options.

One thing is for sure, 'N Sync will be putting their fashion sense to good use. They've signed a unique contract with a licensing company to design a line of sports and active wear. Winterland, the same company that created and marketed much of the 'N Sync merchandise that was sold at their concerts, was taken aback by the success of the group and decided to expand their working relationship with the band. The initial 'N Sync line offered T-shirts, hats, key chains, posters, and calendars, most of which is still available through the group's fan club.

The new stuff, to be designed by Justin, JC, Lance, Chris, and Joey themselves, should be the best yet. "This sensational group will help us design a line of clothing that reflects their clean, All-American image," explained a spokesperson for Winterland. Considering the personal styles of Chris and Justin, there could be an 'N Sync bandanna or hockey jersey in the works. Let's just hope Joey doesn't get too much input in the designs, or else half the country will be parading around in tight zipper pants and purple-hair shirts.

Following Up a Winner

Most likely, as they've discussed, they will begin work on another album. Their debut album was released in Europe a year before it was brought to America and went on to be certified gold in eight different countries and later, multi-platinum in both the U.S. and Canada. How do you follow up an act like that? By following the same formula of talent + desire = winner and adding a dose of experience. "It's going to get a little bigger," Justin warns. "We're just stepping up, moving to the next level," Justin told *Teen Beat* magazine.

Unfortunately and tragically, Denniz Pop, the renowned producer who'd previously worked with Robyn and Ace of Base, and was largely responsible for the hits "Tearin' Up My Heart" and "I Want You Back," passed away in September 1998. However, pop genius Johnny Wright and songwriter Max Martin are still around, and the 'N Sync guys are now older, wiser, and more prepared. Plus, now that the guys have made a name for themselves, they'll be able to attract some of the best writers, producers, and arrangers in the music business to work on their next album.

You can bet that Justin, JC, Lance, Chris, and Joey will take more of a hands-on approach with the new CD. With some serious studio time under their belts now, the guys are ready to try their hand at some producing, arranging, and even songwriting. As for the style of music featured on the next record, we'll have to wait and see. However, at the KIIS-FM Wango Tango benefit concert in California, Chris spilled to a reporter, "It will probably be R&B. It depends how we are feeling at the time—what kind of songs we feel like writing."

Collaborations with other artists is also a possibility for the next record. Already since the release and subsequent success of their debut, 'N Sync was able to team up with R&B sensation Ginuwine. In the earlier part of 1998 the group teamed up with Ginuwine to record the song "Don't Take Your Love Away." The song could possibly be on 'N Sync's next album, but as JC told *Tiger Beat* magazine, "It's really a project. We don't know that it's going to be on an album." In the same interview, Justin and Lance expressed an interest in collaborating with young country singer LeAnn Rimes on a song. "LeAnn with 'N Sync would be a cool mixture," Justin said.

Video Sneak Peek

"I Drive Myself Crazy," which is a track on the American version of *'N Sync,* but not on the original European version, was released as a single in Germany last fall as a special thank-you to the fans who helped launch 'N Sync. The single was accompanied by a unique video shot in Malibu, California, that featured some rather unusual costume changes—even by Joey's standards. "In Europe they've had 'I Want You Back' and 'Tearin' Up My Heart' and this album for a long time, so it's time we gave them some new stuff," JC explained in *All-Stars* magazine.

The video tells the story of an important audition for a new band to play at a big show. Throughout the video, four completely different bands, all played by 'N Sync in costume, try out for the judges. First, Justin, JC, Lance, Chris, and Joey come out as the Jackson 5, in giant wigs and wearing '70s clothes. Then they appear as the Spice Girls, dressed in bright-colored, revealing outfits and platform shoes. Next they come out as a heavy-duty rock band, before finally performing as themselves, and, of course, getting the gig! Stay tuned to see if the video for "I Drive Myself Crazy" winds up on MTV, or if the song ends up being their fourth single off of *'N Sync.*

As for the group's long-range plans, they feel strongly about their future together. "We realize we have such a clique together; this works," Chris told *Billboard* magazine. "I hope we're still touring five years down the line, but I know we'll be together whether it's as producers or as performers. Wouldn't that be great, if the five of us were producing for a new group just coming out? We'd be just as happy." So would your fans, Chris.

Message to the Fans

As 'N Sync's first whirlwind year came to a close, the group had a fan base that seemed to multiply with every concert and appearance. The group's fan club had to more than double its staff to keep up with the bushels of fan mail it was getting every day. "Yeah, it's growing rapidly," Justin told *Teen Beat* magazine. "We're very pleased with the progress we've made. We're nothing but happy and we love our fans."

In the same feature, JC had a message for the group's fans. "We'll be around for a while, so hang with us."

Justin, meanwhile, had a message for 'N Sync manager Johnny Wright. "Hold on to your hat, 'cause this ride has just gotten started!"

12

which 'N Sync guy is right for you?

Let's just say, hypothetically, that you win a big radio contest and the prize is a date with one of the guys from 'N Sync. About two hours after you get the news that you won, after you're done screaming, jumping up and down, and calling all of your friends, you realize something. How on earth are you going to decide which 'N Sync guy will be your dream date?

Apparently, you have all five to choose from as they are all available. When 'N Sync was in Disney World in May 1998, a fan asked if any of them was single. Lance answered, "Well, guess what? We're all single right now and we're looking real hard." Meanwhile, Justin, the little Romeo that he is, responded, "How old are you?"

Lance is such a sweet guy and he has those striking sea green eyes. Joey's charming and seems like he'd be so much fun to hang out with. JC is so polite and he has that killer bod. Chris would crack you up and Justin would melt you with his smile. It's a near impossible choice, but, remember, you can't have 'em all! Check out this breakdown of the romantic side of each guy from 'N Sync and then you decide who would make the best boyfriend for you.

Justin

You've probably been head over heels for seventeen-year-old Justin Timberlake ever since you saw the video for "Tearin' Up My Heart." His boyish good looks are irresistible and he has a quiet confidence about him that's very appealing. Since he's the youngest member of 'N Sync, Justin may be sort of new to the romance scene.

Justin says he's never been in love, but, as he told *16* magazine, "I've been infatuated and had a few crushes. I'm not waiting for it to happen, but I won't run away from it when it does!"

Don't worry, Justin, there aren't too many girls who'd *let* you run away.

His ideal woman would be "confident, humble, sensitive, and with a good sense of humor," and on a first date with a girl, Justin says he'd try to "sweep her off her feet." In an America Online interview, JC said, "Justin's a real charmer, the ladies love him."

- **first girlfriend:** fifth grade
- **first kiss:** fifth grade
- **first date:** sixth grade
- **first time fell in love:** "not yet"
- **celebrity crush:** "I left my heart in Sweden. Robyn's from Sweden and she's the cutest thing and she's friendly, so you've got to move there."

Justin is an Aquarian born January 31. Many astrologers consider Aquarius to be the most richly endowed and highly developed of all signs. In fact, more world leaders, celebrities, and professional athletes have been born under this sign than any other. As a famous, talented, and multi-dimensional performer, Justin fits right in. Typical to his sign, Justin is a spontaneous individual with an imaginative mind. Although Aquarians can be a bit rebellious, they are usually gentle-hearted and lucky in love. Aquarians often look for a significant other who is their friend above all else.

JC

You get to go on a virtual date with twenty-two-year-old JC Chasez every time the "I Want You Back" video is on. When he pulls up in the convertible it's easy to imagine it's *you* getting into the car. Of course, you probably wouldn't break up with good guy JC the way the brunette in the video does!

"I was pretty close [to being in love] once, but I was only 15 and so was she," JC confided in *TV Hits Australia* magazine. "Her name was Francy. She was a beautiful girl inside and out, but it was only a teenage thing. We left each other because I had to move away. Aw, it was sad."

That's how sweet JC is. He's a well-mannered, decent human being and it doesn't hurt that he's famous and really handsome too. Looks aren't as important to JC, who says, "I like all sorts of girls." JC says his ideal woman would be "confident, patient, and outgoing, with a sense of humor," and that on a first date he'd take her to "see a flick or a show, then find a place to talk." Does that sound romantic enough for you?

- **first girlfriend:** first grade
- **first kiss:** first grade
- **first date:** seventh grade
- **first time fell in love:** fourteen years old
- **celebrity crush:** "My favorites would be Naomi Campbell 'cause she's absolutely beautiful, and I'm pretty keen on Michelle Pfeiffer—she's gorgeous. I especially liked her as Catwoman."

JC is, in many ways, a typical Leo. This August 8 birthday boy is a natural-born leader who is magnetic and inspirational to others.

Other characteristics of Leos include ambition, enthusiasm, determination, dignity, generosity, and warmth. However, Leos are far from perfect and can be bossy, arrogant, and neglectful of others. JC doesn't seem to fit any of those descriptions, but then, astrology is an inexact science. On the romantic front, Leos are generally drawn to people who are physically attractive. Once in relationships, they tend to be affectionate, supportive, and loyal.

Lance

It's easy to get lost in Lance Bass's eyes. The nineteen-year-old has transparent yellow-green eyes that almost glow in the dark and could easily hypnotize you. Luckily, it's not as dangerous as it sounds, since Lance is a kind, soft-spoken guy—the kind you'd let date your sister, if you could stand the jealousy.

"I've had girlfriends but afterward realized it wasn't love," Lance confessed to *Teen Machine* magazine. (Not to worry, Lance. Your time will come!) And from what Joey says,

Lance isn't so shy with the ladies. "He's pretty good. We call him 'Stealth' 'cause he sits and watches before he moves in."

When a reporter for *16* magazine asked Lance if he had a girlfriend he answered, "I wish." He's not as picky as the other guys either. His ideal woman "has to be fun loving and have good morals," though he's also said he looks for a girl who's honest and innocent. Lance says he's a sucker for a girl with pretty eyes. On dates, Lance thinks movies and dinners are overrated. Instead he prefers to do something more "adventurous."

- **first girlfriend:** "Bethany Dukes in kindergarten"
- **first kiss:** fourth grade
- **first date:** Kerri Martin, December 1991
- **first time fell in love:** "never"
- **celebrity crush:** "Jennifer Aniston 'cause I love her hair, her face, and her innocent looks. I try to watch *Friends* whenever I can."

Born May 4, Lance is a Taurus. On the upside this typically makes him kind, gentle, honest, loyal, patient, and a good listener. Taureans are also determined workers who are creative, practical, and organized. However, the term "stubborn bull" comes from this sign, and most Taureans would sooner argue until blue in the face than admit they're wrong. One other negative trait often found in Taureans is that they get jealous easily. In the romance department, a male Taurus is likely to seek out an attractive partner who will remain loyal.

Chris

As a fun-loving free spirit with a great sense of humor, twenty-seven-year-old Chris Kirkpatrick would be a lot of fun on a date. Of course it doesn't hurt his appeal that he's talented, famous, and cute as can be, either. What makes him really irresistible is the fact that he really knows how to treat a lady. You see, from growing up with four halfsisters, Chris can really understand a girl's feelings a bit better than the average guy.

"I've fallen in love twice," Chris admitted in

TV Hits magazine. "The last time was with a girl called Catherine. It lasted three months and that was my longest relationship." Although Chris is the oldest member of 'N Sync, he is by no means looking to settle down at this time. The rigors of touring don't really afford him the time right now. But, still, he does have an ideal woman in mind—she would be "very funny" and "spontaneous." Chris says he looks for "a cute face and a good personality" and that he likes to take dates to the beach.

- **first girlfriend:** Nicole in second grade
- **first kiss:** Amy, during a game of tag
- **first date:** Kelly in high school
- **first time fell in love:** Kelly in high school
- **celebrity crush:** "I'm into [No Doubt's] Gwen Stefani—I love her!"

Libras are extremely charming, likable, and outgoing people who enjoy the finer things in life. If that sounds a bit like Chris, that's because he's a Libra, born October 17. Libras are very peaceful people who shun violence and even like to try to keep peace among their family and friends. Love is very important to Libras, who tend to be emotional, sometimes to a fault. Because Libras are also usually highly intelligent, they sometimes have an inner struggle between what they love to do and what they think they should do. Libras can also sometimes be show-offs. When it comes to relationships, Libras are romantic, spontaneous, and thoughtful.

Joey

Twenty-one-year-old Joey Fatone is as charming as they come. Even his band mates say he's a big-time flirt. Joey says it's "a good way to get to know people," but Chris leaked his secret to *Teen Beat* magazine. "He likes the label. When girls hear he's flirtatious, they're like, 'Hi, Joey, how are you?' It works for him."

Joey would likely take a girl dancing on a date. Keep in mind though that while his moves on the dance floor may impress you, some of the duds he dons may embarrass you! But don't be afraid to tell him as much. Joey says he likes a girl who speaks her mind. Looks-wise, Joey says he doesn't really have a specific type, though he says he's first attracted to a girl's smile. His ideal woman would be "fun, outgoing, and honest. She has to be herself too."

"I've had really strong feelings for a girl called Dinay, but it wasn't love," Joey explained. "We went out for about four months at high school. She left to go to college and that was the end of it." There's plenty more fish in the sea for a guy who's upbeat, friendly, and world famous.

- **first girlfriend:** Jenny, ten years old
- **first kiss:** Lisa, eleven years old
- **first date:** movies, thirteen years old
- **first time fell in love:** "not really"
- **celebrity crush:** "There are so many, I could go on forever! But I've liked Demi Moore for a while, ever since I saw *Ghost.* I don't mind her with long or short hair."

Like Justin, Joey also fits many of the characteristics of his Aquarius sign. Born on January

28, Joey is an idealist and a humanitarian, two of the most telling qualities of an Aquarian. If Joey fits some of the other traits of his sign, then he may also be a philosophical thinker and a problem solver with a great memory. On the downside, Aquarians don't like to follow routines and often procrastinate. In relationships, Aquarians are tender and sincere and will make sacrifices to maintain harmony. On the flip side, a male Aquarian's romantic interest may sometimes feel neglected because she's competing with so many of his friends.

Now that you've had a chance to examine your options, have you come to a decision? Whether you decided on Justin, JC, Lance, Chris, or Joey, you can't go wrong. You're bound to have a great time, but just be sure to bring a camera so your friends will believe you!

13

numerology

'N Sync fans probably think the fine five are the number one group in the world. And on the cutie scale, they rate a perfect 10. But, in numerology terms, Justin's an eight and Lance is a seven, while Joey, Chris, and JC are all sixes. So, what does that mean? Originally developed by the Babylonians thousands of years ago, numerology is simply a way of determining someone's personality type based on their name. The method calls for assigning each person a number from one through nine, determined by the number of letters in his or her full name (middle names are included). It's a pretty easy way to figure out what type you fit into. Numerology can also be used for family, friends, classmates, crushes, and, in this case, favorite bands.

After using the method on the 'N Sync guys, it was determined that three of the guys, Joey,

Chris, and JC, are sixes, while Lance is a seven and Justin is an eight. This doesn't mean that Justin is the best (though some of you may feel this way), but it does mean that Joey, Chris, and JC have more than a few things in common—a good thing, considering how much time these guys spend together! Try it out on your name to see how in sync you are with 'N Sync.

Here's how to do it. Write out your full name, and then match the letters up with the following chart, as with the 'N Sync examples given here.

1	2	3	4	5	6	7	8	9
A	B	C	D	E	F	G	H	I
J	K	L	M	N	O	P	Q	R
S	T	U	V	W	X	Y	Z	

JUSTIN RANDALL TIMBERLAKE
131295 9154133 2942593125

JOSHUA SCOTT CHASEZ
161831 13622 381158

JAMES LANCE BASS
11451 31535 2111

CHRISTOPHER ALAN KIRKPATRICK
38991267859 1315 29927129932

JOSEPH ANTHONY FATONE
161578 1528657 612655

The next step is to add up all of the corresponding numbers. You should come up with 89 for Justin, 60 for JC, 34 for Lance, 87 for Joey, and 132 for Chris and his really long name. The final step in this simple equation is to add the two numbers together until you get a single digit. With Justin, for example, 8 + 9 = 17, and then 1 + 7 = 8. This makes Justin an 8. Do the same for JC, Joey, and Chris and you come up with 6, and Lance is a lucky 7.

What does this say about the 'N Sync guys? For one thing, since three of them share the same number, they obviously make quite a team. Since Joey, JC, and Chris are all sixes, let's examine that number first.

SIX—In numerology, a personality type six is generally kind and generous. Six is an ideal best friend or sibling. Sixes also tend to keep an open mind, always inviting new suggestions and ideas. On the downside, sixes tend to be a bit naive and are sometimes too quick to trust people. Sixes get along well with other sixes (you know that's true, the way these guys can crack each other up!), as well as with eights and nines. That's good news for Justin, who tallies up as an eight.

SEVEN—The most reserved and quiet of all the numbers is seven and, appropriately, the shiest member of 'N Sync, Lance, is a seven. However, sevens warm up around people they know well, and aren't afraid to share their feelings. Because of this, sevens make trustworthy companions. On the flip side, sevens can be oversensitive and sometimes don't handle constructive criticism very well. Still, sevens get along with everybody but ones, so they're never short of friends.

EIGHT—Outgoing, adventurous, and full of energy is the best way to describe an eight.

(Sound a bit like a certain blond pop star?) An eight is an original person who's always offering up new and exciting ideas. Eights give it all they've got, but when the work is done, watch out! Eights can be party animals. On the flip side, eights tend to be spendthrifts (Justin admits that shopping is one of his favorite pastimes). Eights are compatible with threes and sixes.

Are you compatible with Justin or Lance? Do your numbers add up to six like Joey, JC, or Chris? Figure it out. Here are descriptions of the traits for all the numbers.

Ones are natural-born leaders. They stay motivated through thick and thin, but sometimes bite off more than they can chew. Ones live for the spotlight, but they should share it once in a while because others can become resentful. But everybody needs friends, and some can overlook a few bad points in a person. That's where numbers two and four come in.

Twos make great, trustworthy companions who will stop at nothing to help out the ones they love. If your best pal's a two she'll likely take care of your pet while you're on vacation or bring over the assignment you missed when you were out sick. Twos tend to get too wrapped up in their own emotions sometimes though. Luckily, fours and sevens are there to cheer them up.

Threes are a complicated bunch. They can adapt well to new situations and surroundings and are usually charming and friendly. However, they can be a bit bossy at times, turning off potential new pals. Other than fours and fives, threes don't get along very well with others.

Fours are incredible people who are serious and responsible, but still maintain a good sense of humor. They are honest to a fault and make great buddies too. So, what's not to like? Fours can have a real knack for saying the wrong thing at the wrong time. This doesn't seem to bother twos, fives, and eights. A four's best friend is usually a one.

Fives are typically deep thinkers who love to get extra-involved in their projects. Fives are perfectionists who feel like they must always do the best job they possibly can, even if it means putting in overtime or making sacrifices. The problem is, they sometimes forget their friends on the way to achieving their goals. Ones and fours usually count at least one five among their closest friends.

Sixes are guys like JC Chasez, Chris Kirkpatrick, and Joey Fatone. If you're cool like that, check out the traits listed for these three 'N Sync guys.

If your number is **seven**, look back at the numerology traits listed for Lance. You and Lansten are like two peas in a pod!

If you're a crazy **eight**, check out the low-down on Justin.

Nines are kindhearted people, in the broad sense. A nine would go to great lengths to start a school fund-raiser or get involved in charity work, but at the same time, forget that their brother or sister needs them. Nines enjoy a good laugh and can be loads of fun to be around. Fours, sevens, and eights all make good pals.

14

websites & fan mail

Do you care enough to send the guys from 'N Sync your very best? There are many ways you can contact Justin, JC, Lance, Chris, and Joey. Whether you're looking for the latest updates, gossip, or a chance to meet other fans, the Internet is a virtual playground for 'N Sync fans. 'N Sync's official website (www.nsync.com) is the first place you should look for up-to-date information on the band. Surf onto the above address for the latest news on 'N Sync, as well as fan club info, music and videos, tour dates, bio data, chat rooms, band e-mail, and links to other websites.

In a *Bop* magazine feature the 'N Sync guys 'fessed up to spending hours on-line. Chris and JC both said they respond to fan e-mail messages whenever they can. "When we are busy, we can't sit down and talk with the fans," Chris said, "but it's much easier for me to get in touch with them this way. I read all the e-mail and I try to write back to as many as possible."

But that's getting harder and harder to do as the group gets more popular and gains more fans. "When I write back, all of a sudden I'll get like a billion hits the next day because I actually replied," JC added.

Joey has given the Internet the old college try, but he says his slow typing makes it frustrating for him. "I'm a horrible typist. I'm just like, 'plink, plink,' and before I know it, four hours are gone already."

Meanwhile, Lance is busy hanging out in a different part of cyberspace. "Chat rooms are so cool," he told *Bop* magazine. "Especially if you go into your own chat room. I absolutely love talking to everybody. If I go on-line, like six hours pass, but you don't even know how long you've been on it." Careful what you say out there in computer land, though—Lance might be listening. He admits to sometimes eavesdropping on chats without participating!

It won't be long before Justin joins the other guys on the Internet. "As soon as I get my own laptop, then I'm going to be on it all the time," Justin said.

Aside from 'N Sync's official website, there are also more fan-produced websites and links than you can shake a stick at, with plenty of links to chat rooms and e-mail addresses so you can swap info with other 'N Sync fanatics. If, on the other hand, you wouldn't know the Information Superhighway from Route 66, there's also a snail-mail address where you can send fan letters, poems, drawings, and birthday cards. Here are a few things to keep in mind.

1. Use caution when surfing the net. Checking out amateur websites and meeting other 'N Sync fans on-line is a great way to gather information and swap thoughts and ideas on your favorite group. However, not everything you read on the Internet is accurate. After all, you don't have to be an 'N Sync insider or even a computer expert to post materials about them on the Internet.

Anyone with 50 dollars and a little hi-tech know-how can fire up a website. Never give out your full name, address, or phone number to someone you've only met on-line.

2. If you choose to send regular fan mail to 'N Sync, remember that your letter will be one of thousands the group will receive that week. Use your imagination to make your letter stand out from all the rest. A brightly colored envelope will stand out from all the white ones. You can show the guys you put a lot of effort into your letter by gluing sequins or sparkles to the envelope or spicing it up with some stickers or drawings. Sending a birthday card is another way to grab 'N Sync's attention. The guys are on the road so much that when one of their birthdays rolls around, there usually isn't time for parties and cake cutting with family and friends. A well-timed birthday card from a fan could be just the thing to make them smile, and maybe even grab a pen and respond to your letter!
3. Be very patient. Don't expect to hear back from 'N Sync right away. Traveling the

world, spending hours rehearsing, performing, and doing interviews doesn't leave much time for anything other than sleep. 'N Sync loves their fans and will respond to fan mail, but, until their schedule calms down a bit, it may take a while.

4. Don't expect to receive a personalized letter. Justin, JC, Lance, Chris, and Joey get nearly a million fan letters a month from all around the world, not to mention thousands of e-mails and website hits. In order to keep up, the boys would have to write thousands of responses per week, and that wouldn't leave much time for what they do best—make music!

Official fan club: 'N Sync
P.O. Box 692109
Orlando, FL 32869–2109

Record company: 'N Sync
c/o RCA Records
1540 Broadway
New York, NY 10036

'N Sync
c/o RCA Records
6363 Sunset Blvd.
Hollywood, CA 90028

Management: 'N Sync
c/o Trans Continental
Entertainment
7380 Sand Lake Rd.
Suite 350
Orlando, FL 32189

Official Internet Website:
http://www.nsync.com

RCA Records:
http://www.bmg.com/rca/artists/nsync

Unofficial Websites:
www.nsyncworld.com
www.angelfire.com/fl/justeensync.html
www.geocities.com/sunsetstrip/towers/6354
www.geocities.com/timessquare/stadium/3713
www.geocities.com/sunsetstrip/stage/5955

www.geocities.com/sunsetstrip/4527
www.geocities.com/timessquare/stadium/1347
www.geocities.com/paris/cafe/7063/nsyncaol.html

There are nearly one hundred amateur websites devoted to 'N Sync. Many feature photos, bio data, faves, background information, song lyrics, and, of course, rumors. For a complete listing, use a search engine, like Yahoo, Excite, Lycos, or Dogpile and first narrow your search to music/artists. If you're on America Online, you can also try "keyword: N Sync." These are a few of the best unofficial 'N Sync sites on the Web at press time.

15

test your 'N Sync knowledge

After reading this book, and probably every article on 'N Sync you could find, you should be a certified 'N Sync expert. Let's see how much you really know. After you take this test, check the answers on page 161 (remember, no cheating!). Then turn to page 164 to see how you measure up to other 'N Sync fans.

1. Who was the fifth and final member to join 'N Sync?
2. Who thought up the name 'N Sync?
3. What city is considered the band's home base?
4. What record label are they on?
5. Who is the band's manager?

6. Which two members of 'N Sync got their start on *The Mickey Mouse Club?*
7. Which two got started at Universal Studios theme park?
8. In the "I Want You Back" video, which two band members play one-on-one basketball?
9. Who drives the convertible in the video?
10. Which of the following does not take place in the video?

    (A) Jet Skiing (B) volleyball (C) shooting pool (D) a water fight
11. Who gets pushed into the water?
12. Where does the "Tearin' Up My Heart" video take place?
13. Which band member appears on a bed?
14. Which of the following does not appear in the video?

    (A) punching bag (B) weight bench (C) full-length mirror (D) treadmill
15. Who holds an acoustic guitar at the end of the video?
16. Who is the principal songwriter of both 'N *Sync* hits, "I Want You Back" and "Tearin' Up My Heart"?

17. What singer/songwriter originally made the song "Sailing" a hit back in 1980?
18. Where was *'N Sync* recorded?
19. Which two members of 'N Sync sing lead on "I Want You Back" and "Tearin' Up My Heart"?
20. Which band member hits the high notes best?
21. Who has the deepest voice in the band?
22. Which 'N Sync guy collects Superman memorabilia?
23. Who wanted to be an astronaut?
24. Who is considered the most serious member of the group?
25. Who is the youngest member of 'N Sync?
26. Who is the oldest?
27. Who's been known to wear the most ridiculous outfits to go out dancing in?
28. How many songs are on the American version of *'N Sync?*
29. How many are on the European version?
30. What song on the debut album did 'N Sync co-write?
31. What was the release date of *'N Sync?*

32. True or false? The debut album went platinum
33. True or false? "I Want You Back" hit number 1 on the *Billboard* singles chart
34. What was the name of their first Disney Channel special?
35. True or false? The special got such good ratings that The Disney Channel re-aired it six more times over the summer
36. Which televised beauty pageant show did 'N Sync perform in?
37. What record store did 'N Sync help open with a city tour and live performance?
38. What New York City landmark did 'N Sync appear at as part of a Twix promotion?
39. What song was released as 'N Sync's third single in America?
40. What late dance producer, who previously worked with Robyn and Ace of Base, produced and co-wrote "Tearin' Up My Heart" and "I Want You Back"?
41. Who did 'N Sync open for on the first portion of their American tour?
42. In what city did 'N Sync kick off the headlining portion of their U.S. tour?

43. Who opened for 'N Sync on their American tour?
44. Which of the following talk shows did 'N Sync appear on?
    (A) *The View* (B) *The Ricki Lake Show* (C) *The Tonight Show* (D) *Live! with Regis & Kathie Lee* (E) all of the above
45. True or false? 'N Sync appeared on a float in the Macy's Thanksgiving Day Parade
46. What was the magical day when the 'N Sync holiday album, home video, and official book all came out?
47. What is the name of the holiday album?
48. What four classic Christmas songs did 'N Sync cover on the album?
49. How many original songs did they do on the album?
50. What TV special was 'N Sync a part of on December 25, 1998?

Answers to the 'N Sync Knowledge Test

1. Lance Bass
2. Justin's mom
3. Orlando, Florida

4. RCA
5. Johnny Wright
6. Justin Timberlake and JC Chasez
7. Chris Kirkpatrick and Joey Fatone
8. Justin Timberlake and Chris Kirkpatrick
9. JC Chasez
10. B
11. Lance Bass
12. in a warehouse
13. Justin Timberlake
14. D
15. JC Chasez
16. Max Martin
17. Christopher Cross
18. Stockholm, Sweden, and Munich, Germany
19. Justin Timberlake and JC Chasez
20. Chris Kirkpatrick
21. Lance Bass
22. Joey Fatone
23. Lance Bass
24. JC Chasez
25. Justin Timberlake
26. Chris Kirkpatrick

27. Joey Fatone
28. 13
29. 14
30. "Giddy Up"
31. March 24, 1998
32. True: by the time you read this, it may have hit triple-platinum
33. False: the single went gold but peaked at #13
34. *'N Sync In Concert*
35. True: it turned out to be one of the highest rated shows in the network's history!
36. the Miss Teen USA Pageant
37. the Virgin Mega Store in New York City
38. the World Trade Center
39. "God Must Have Spent a Little More Time on You"
40. Denniz Pop
41. Janet Jackson
42. Orlando, Florida
43. Brittany Spears and Wild Orchid
44. E
45. True
46. November 10, 1998

47. *Home for Christmas*
48. "The First Noel," "The Christmas Song," "This Christmas," and "O Holy Night"
49. eight
50. ABC's *Walt Disney World Christmas Special*

Scoring

Tally up your score and see how big an 'N Sync fan you are!

38–50 correct: You rock! You know almost as much about 'N Sync as the guys in the band do!

25–37 correct: Darn good. You're definitely down with 'N Sync.

15–24 correct: Not bad. You might know a thing or two about Justin, JC, Lance, Chris and Joey, but not enough to be an 'N Sync fanatic.

10–14 correct: You've got some 'N Sync homework to do. Better start stocking up on teen mags and spending some more time on-line.

0–9 correct: Who are you kidding?! If your score falls in this category, you probably can't even tell the 'N Sync guys apart from one another.

About the Author

Matt Netter is a freelance writer who works and lives in New York City. He is also the author of several other young reader entertainment books, including the *New York Times* bestseller *Zac Hanson: Totally Zac.* He's currently at work on a fictional Christmas story loosely based on his childhood.